Gifted
by magic

Diana Marie DuBois

Pirates Alley

Diana Marie DuBois

Published by Three Danes Publishing L.L.C.

THREE DANES

PUBLISHING

Cover art by Anya Kelleye
http://www.anyakelleye.com/
Cover photo stock
Edited by Maxine Horton Bringenberg
Guardian logo created by P and N Graphics

My Acknowledgements and Thanks

~Thanks to my street team, you girls are the best.

~Anita, you are the best PA ever, and baby girl loves you.

~My supportive and wonderful parents, I am blessed every day knowing I am your daughter.

~Anya Kelleye, okay this is a given. I have the best cover artist ever.

~All lovers of the fur baby kind, this book is for you. Animals bring joy to our lives. Ever wondered what they thought? Here's your chance to imagine.

~My wonderful spell caster Mary K Hensley, thanks for writing up a spell whenever and whatever time I message you.

~Cutting Muse Blog. Makayla, you are awesome.

~My fans; you guys rock.

~ A big shout out to Mary Nancy Smith for always fixing those nasty little headers and footers. Muah

~I would like to thank one special fan, Annabelle Stauffacher. I hope you enjoy Athena's second book, sweetheart.

Dedication

To the most wonderful Great Danes I could ask for. Thank you Lily, Luna, and Max for inspiring me to write a story told in a dog's POV. You three have gifted me with something I will never lose. "Love"

Note to readers

Athena and Rosie are both growing into their powers. This series is by far the most fun for me to write. Athena's antics bring a smile to my face. In this story you will see that she meets many new characters that you don't see in *Voodoo Vows*. They were in that story, but you never saw them because at the time they were only seen by Athena. She sees Baron Samedi and Papa Legba, who are loa of voodoo. Being a city of decadence I plan on showing that side of the city through the drag queen community. These people are truly talented, the first two I introduce are Eureeka and Philomena. You see them only for a moment, but don't worry, they will show up again. I met Eureeka through Facebook and instantly fell in love with all her posts, so I decided to write her a character. Philomena is named after my mom's hairdresser, you know we love you Phil. I mean after all, the Quarter is nothing without its drag queens.

Glossary

~ **Baron Samedi**— the loa of voodoo who watches over the dead.

~ **Box with moving pics**— TV

~ **Contraption on wheels**— street car

~ **Flea bag**— Julian

~ **Long strings of balls**— Mardi Gras beads

~ **Large rolling boxes**— Mardi Gras floats

~ **Noisy thing that raced around on tracks**— Julians snoring

~ **Ooey gooey dessert**— king cake

~ **Papa Legba**— the loa of voodoo who you meet at the crossroads and must speak with in order to speak to other loa.

~ **Spirit Guide**— a special person who is a ghost to help Athena through her life.

~ **Reflection thingy**— mirror

~ **Sweet flower**— magnolia

Table of Contents

Evil Has Come....

"Those who don't believe in magic will never find it."
    Roald Dahl

A tale of a tail where magic flows.
Words in which strength and power grows.
To get the story the focus to shift.
We learn how powerful magic is a gift.

a new life

fter Alexander dropped me off, my life and the protection of my witch started. As she cuddled me I sensed she was sad and yet had no idea why. The girl who sat beside us was the one I had seen in Alisa's magic ball, and I instantly liked her. *Friend of my witch, you remind me of someone I knew back in Germany. She showed me you in her magic orb.* I tried putting the thoughts into her head, but she never uttered a reply. In seconds I became worried that no one would hear me, though I guessed this girl wasn't a witch or a gypsy.

As I sat on the scratchy material that covered my witches lap, I saw her pull something from a hidden spot. The same wetness came from her eyes that had come from the households' eyes when Karl had left us. I knew I must comfort my witch. *It will be okay, Mom, I'm here for you.*

She read the words that were on the paper, and I knew something was wrong. *Oh no*, I thought. That nice lady who had visited us in Germany—who I now realized smelled similar to my witch—was gone like Karl. I nestled even closer to Rosie, trying to tell her I was so sorry, and that I felt her pain.

After Rosie and her friend, who I quickly learned was called Jahane, got up, my witch asked me, "Are you ready to go, little one?" I jumped up and ran around in circles at the familiar name, though I knew it wasn't my true name. *Yes yes*! Then I grinned up at my witch.

I bounded in front of and behind the two girls, excited for my new life. Rosie picked me up and we walked into a building. As the door opened, I heard a strange noise above us and tilted my head. My nose instantly smelled the most amazing scents...some ever so similar to those in cook's kitchen, but also other smells I couldn't wait to discover. A woman looked up at us and smiled. When she walked around her gaze stopped on me, and I knew she knew what I was. Excitement flowed through me.

Rosie let me down and my paws scratched at the floor in the direction of all the shelves and boxes. I pulled a rope thing from a box and chewed it, then growled at it when it wouldn't play with me. Getting bored quickly, I kicked it away and trotted over to a corner. A funny feeling circled around my nose and I sneezed.

"Bless you, Guardian." I turned to the sound and saw a lady smiling at me. *Thank you.* I tried to talk to her but she also couldn't hear me, much like cook.

I followed them into the back, where I paid close attention to my surroundings. As I listened to them speaking, I realized my witch did not believe in magic or that she was a witch. Sadness overcame me, but along with it came fear that flowed around the room. I knew I needed to somehow get her to believe.

my name is…

e watched as my witch's best friend left us, then I jumped from Rosie's arms. *Mom, what will we do now? Play?* I tried talking to her again, but nothing. I would keep trying. She stood there rubbing her head, and a part of me hoped I was getting through.

So I attempted to climb the steps. One, two, and three. *Oops.* I felt myself tumble backward. *Come on,* I told myself, *you can do it.* Finally, after a couple of attempts, I made it. Up at the top I sat and waited for her. She climbed the steps, and when she stood in front of me I inclined my head at her. *It's about time.*

After she'd unlocked the door, I stepped over the threshold, looked around, and saw a strange box. I flicked it on with my mind. Moving pictures appeared and I sat on my haunches, amazed. Finally I sprawled my body out, my legs behind me and my head on my paws, and watched. After

Rosie had come inside, she placed all my goodies on the floor. I went over to her and nudged her. *Mom, I'm hungry.*

She looked down at me. "What is it, huh girl?"

I bumped the dog food bag and almost tipped it over. "Oh, you are hungry, girl." Once she'd poured the kibble into my bowl, I gobbled it up. Love and magic flowed through the soft touch of my witch petting me as I ate.

With my belly full I trudged off after my new mom as she entered another room. In it was a huge bed, and as she got into it, I whimpered. "Come on, little girl, let's get some sleep. We have a big day ahead of us tomorrow."

Throughout the night my mom tossed and turned. I couldn't wake her, and her moving about scared me. I sat up in the bed and watched her intently.

The edge of the bed dipped down a bit, and I glanced over to see a hazy figure of a beautiful woman. Her voice drifted into my head. *Little one, she'll be okay. I promise. It is one of her powers. She must see it all.*

I nudged Rosie with my head. *But she seems to be frightened.*

She petted me, her ghostly hand becoming solid as it touched me and comforted me. *She is, but it is only one of her powers surfacing more. The evil must be close. You must keep an eye on her. But remember, not all evil will show itself.*

Beside my witch with my head on her chest, I hoped to settle her somehow. As my eyes grew heavy I began to drift off to sleep.

Go to sleep, little one, the voice said.

The warmth that comforted me was a welcome feeling. I belly crawled under the covers until I was close enough to lick my witch's face. Her eyes opened one at a time, which gave me an excuse to slink closer to her. Because I knew she hadn't slept well, I stilled for a second. She'd done nothing but shift about in the bed all night.

"So what should I call you?" my witch pondered.

I cocked my head at her as I watched the intent look in her eyes, then she burst out, "I'll call you Athena." The soft sound of her laughter made me feel at home.

I love it. I tried to convey my love of this new name, but she still couldn't hear me. The name had a strong and loyal sound to it.

My new mom scooted off the bed, so I followed her. She knelt on the floor and seemed to be looking for something. She grabbed the fuzzy object before I even had a chance to latch my mouth around it. As she placed her foot in it, I sat back, waiting.

We headed out of the room and down the hallway, which now had my full attention, and I sniffed every nook and cranny I could. I backed away from the last corner I stuck my nose in with something ticklish attached to it. It fell softly to the floor so I decided to chase it, but every time I got close it ran from me. Determined to not let this ball of fluff get away from me, I continued after it.

The melodious voice of my mom pulled me back to reality. "Okay, Athena, let's get some breakfast."

I padded after her. Before long the kitchen aromas floated around me, making my stomach growl. The food hitting my metal bowl alerted me and I ran over, almost knocking her down, and gobbled down every last bit.

As I licked the last bits of stuck on food, a knock sounded on the door. Instantly my hackles rose; evil stood outside the door. *Mom, don't open the door.* I turned to see the door open, and a tall man, the one I'd seen in the crystal ball, stood before me.

I stood still, then slowly growled. Over my rumbles the voice of my mom chastised me for growling at the evil man. *But Mom, he's evil. Watch out, I can sense it.* I tried to get her attention, but she wasn't hearing me.

"Come, Athena." She patted her leg to get me to follow her to the room where we'd slept. "Stay here, girl."

But, Mom—

My words were interrupted as the door shut in front of me. I scratched at the door to get her to open it back up, but got no response. Being ignored, I scrambled up onto the bed, turned around three times, and then settled down with my head on my paws.

After a nap I woke to an empty house, but the bedroom door had been opened. A wave of electricity coursed through my body and my hair stood on end as I headed down the hallway. The moment my nose touched the front door it swung open, and I bounded down the steps and into the courtyard. I wondered where my witch was, and scanned the area. As the thought came to me, warmth spread through me to a spot on my chest. A blur passed by me and flitted around. I barked and barked.

"Shh," the fuzzy woman said to me. I stopped barking, but tilted my head from side to side. The woman seemed familiar to me somehow. A shimmering hand reached out and petted me. "Hello, little one, what's your name? Did she finally name you?"

Athena, I barked.

The see-through figure floated around me then sat down on the steps behind me. "That's a nice name, and one befitting a true Guardian."

You can hear me?

She laughed. "Yes, I can understand your thoughts. Ghosts can do more than others because we balance between the two realms of life and death."

I turned and sat down on my back end. *Wait, you know about Guardians?*

"Of course I do," she said, laughing. "Remember, I visited Alexander and met you."

So what are you, and why do you look different than the others here?

Her kind smile warmed me. "Athena, I'm what is called a ghost. I've died, but instead of moving on I decided to stay on and help my daughter, and eventually you."

You are Rosie's mom. I couldn't believe it. *Are you a Guardian too?*

"No, you are a Guardian. I am here to bring you your guide...your spirit guide, to be exact."

What? Alexander didn't tell me any of this.

"No, he had no idea. When I returned home from Germany after meeting you, I knew you were special. Also, I knew Rosie wouldn't believe right away, so I needed to make sure you didn't get discouraged about that. Soon your spirit guide will come to you."

I plopped my head down on the bottom step, inches from her foot. I wanted to place it on her, but was afraid to since she didn't seem like Rosie.

"Ha ha. Athena, you won't hurt me if you touch me. I can make myself corporeal if needed. Now, do you have any questions for me?"

I popped my head up and one ear flopped over my eye. I stood on all fours and paced as a slew of questions came bubbling out.

"Slow down, Athena," she laughed.

Okay, I have one for now. Will Rosie ever be able to hear me?

"Yes she will, but she has a long road ahead of her. She will need you more than ever. But once she begins to believe in herself and her abilities, she will be able to hear you. Just be patient."

Who will be my spirit guide?

"I will bring him to you soon, Athena."

Before I could ask her another question, I sensed Jahane walking into the courtyard and my new friend disappeared.

"Athena, what are you doing outside? And what in the world are you barking at?"

I turned and ran over to her, almost knocking her down in my excitement.

"Come on, girl, let's get you inside before your mom gets home from the zoo and worries about you." I climbed up the steps behind her. She walked through the wide open door as I followed her. "How did you get out?"

I barked at her. After she checked the house and was confident it was safe, she filled both my food and water bowls. She sat on the sofa while I finished my kibble, flipping the channels on the talking box. I nudged my head up under her hand for her to pet me, then headed back towards Rosie's room.

As I crawled into the bed I heard the door close, and drifted off to sleep with heavy thoughts about who could be my spirit guide.

Doubt or belief

he next day I woke with a new enlightenment...I would try my best to get my witch to hear me. As I sat around I heard rumblings about this thing called Mardi Gras. I knew I needed to find out what it was.

When my mom and I went outside I pranced around, sniffing everyone. When I saw Jahane and Julian approaching, the hair on my back rose. *Mom, watch out, he's evil.* But she didn't hear me so I relented and growled at him. When Jahane reached me she grabbed my leash.

"Come on, girl. You's so coote, let's let them have some alone time."

Jahane dragged me away as I continued to growl, and I knew I would do anything if he hurt Rosie. I glanced around as Jahane and I stood o the sidewalk, the sights and sounds were nothing like in Germany. People were screaming and had their bodies laced with long strings of tiny balls. I knew I must have these same items.

Finally my mom arrived, and the streets were littered with people and these huge boxes holding more people. Strings of balls soared through the air, so I caught some and held on to them. But in all the excitement I sensed an evil that lurked. My witch stood staring at something, though I could not see what had caught her attention. I padded over toward her and bumped her hand with my head. Her hand was rigid as I nudged her. A slightly hazy figure covered all in black shimmered out of sight. As soon as it disappeared, Rosie seemed to calm, though her demeanor was different.

Mom, look at me. Yes, I am looking fine with all these dangling necklaces. She laughed nervously.

The large rolling boxes disappeared and we headed away. As I stepped over all the debris my nose stayed close to the ground, catching all the scents in order to protect my witch. All of a sudden I picked up my head when I smelled Julian. He walked toward us and Rosie ran to him, her worry evident in her voice. But I kept my eyes on him the whole time.

After a few moments we left Jahane and followed Julian up some steps. The odor of river water wafted up and filled my nose with the smells of fish and other things I couldn't identify. Once at the top the wind blew around me and I felt a presence with us, but never saw it. I did know that it wasn't evil. After a man came up and spoke to Julian, I headed off to inspect things. Turning the corner, I saw Rosie's mom and trotted up to her.

"How are you, Athena?"

I'm good. Then sadness rolled through me. *When do you think Rosie will be able to hear me and talk to me?*

"Be patient; she needs to believe in herself."

I sat, swishing my tail like a big fan, and looked up at her. Her brown hair blew in the wind as she smiled at me.

"Athena, I'll be around...why don't you go back to Rosie for now? And don't be too harsh on Julian, he's a good guy. In time you'll learn to trust him, though they both have a long road ahead of them."

I barked as she disappeared slowly before me. I took one more sniff then meandered back to the table. The smells were making my mouth water.

I quietly crawled under the table and sat next to Rosie's feet. They were so involved in each other she'd never noticed I'd been gone. My tummy rumbled and I peeked my head out from under the table and looked up at her.

"Here ya go, Athena."

14

I took the piece of chicken and gobbled it up. *Thanks, Mom.* I tried to push into her head, but nothing. I couldn't lose hope...she had to believe.

My paws carried me a few steps ahead of them as they meandered down the street. When I sensed that they'd stopped in front of the mules that I'd seen when I first arrived here with Alexander, I turned and walked back to them, and watched as Julian helped Rosie into the carriage. He touched me to help me up, but an electrical shock flowed through me. I snarled at him but held back, careful not to bite him since I didn't want to upset my witch.

"Here, let me get her," the nice man standing beside us said. He lifted me up then petted my head. I turned around three times on the floor of the carriage after finding a comfortable spot next to my witch's feet.

As I lay there I started to fall asleep. Visions of my brother Ares plagued me. I missed him and the others so much. Would they be disappointed in me since I was having so much trouble getting my witch to hear me?

A soft female voice spoke to me. *No, Athena, they wouldn't. Give her time, she will hear you.*

The bouncing of the carriage calmed me and I began to fall asleep. As I drifted in and out, trying to keep all my senses on Rosie, the voice told me to let go.

I walked though tall grass and over to a huge tree. Grey strings hung from the branches like nothing I'd seen before. My witch's mother Magnolia came from behind the tree.

"Athena, are you still bothered by my daughter not hearing you?"

I nodded. "Yes, but now something else is bothering me."

"What is it?"

"Why, when Julian touched me, did it feel like a dozen tiny pins were sticking me all at once? I had to be careful not to bite him...I didn't want Rosie upset."

"Oh, Athena. Julian is sick, so to speak, but it's not his fault."

"Will he hurt Rosie?"

"No, he won't. I believe this man loves my daughter. All will be revealed in time. Now wake up, Athena, the ride is over. And just remember, you are doing great. Your brother Ares and Alexander would be proud of you."

The carriage came to a stop and I picked my head up. The nice man picked me up, patted me on the head, and placed me on the ground.

On the walk home, I replayed in my head all I had been told. I knew it would all work out, I just had to be patient. No matter what, though, I'd keep an eye on Julian until I could figure out what was going on with him.

Back at home I ran off into the house and into the bedroom. When Rosie got into bed she picked me up and I curled up beside her.

my witch's birthday

waited impatiently for Rosie to finish getting dressed. When I heard the knock on the door I barked, wishing she would hurry up. I knew Jahane was on the other side of the door, along with Julian.

Rosie came running in and opened the door. It was the funniest sight I'd ever seen. The sound coming from them hurt my ears and I began howling. I sat down and stuck my nose in the air. "Ahoooo." The more they sang, the more I wanted to join in. *Sing more*, I pleaded. "Ahoooo."

"Okay you two, stop it," I heard my witch say.

No Mom. "Ahoooo." I kept singing along with them. Then I started to prance around.

"Come on, Athena, let's go." She ushered the three of us outside. As I followed them, I kept a close eye on Rosie and stayed close to her, almost leaning on her. We boarded some sort of contraption on wheels, and as I hopped on and into a seat next to Jahane, I stuck my head out the window. My tongue flapped in the wind as we moved. I tasted all sorts of bugs...all were a little salty.

When the contraption stopped I looked around. "Athena, it's time to get off." Rosie patted her leg and I jumped off the seat and skidded on the metal floor, almost bumping into another person.

"Ahh, what a cute dog."

I smiled up at them and jumped off the thing on wheels. I followed Rosie, Jahane, and Julian down the street, keeping my nose to the ground. We stopped at a giant door and walked inside, where a giant man picked up my witch and squeezed her. I sat down and watched, waiting to jump in if he hurt her. But he never did. He then saw me, leaned down, and with a giant hand petted me, so I reached up and licked his face. The giant turned to my witch. "If anyone says anything about your dog, you let me know."

She nodded, "Okay, Derrick," then turned to me. "Let's go find Julian and let these two talk." I followed her in, and as I walked through the crowd I looked for anything out of the ordinary. When we reached the table I crawled under it and rested my head on my paws. I growled from under the table at Julian. But then I remembered what my guide had told me.

Before long the room was loud and two people on stage were singing to my witch...my witch. She must really be loved. I wasn't sure what all this was about, but I knew I had to find out.

Athena, they are celebrating my daughter's birthday. I turned around at the voice, but it was in my head.

Her birthday? What is a birthday?

She laughed. *It's when humans or the living celebrate when they were born. They give presents...you, Athena, were my daughter's present from me.* I felt a slight touch along my back, and relished in the movements of her hand.

Do I have a birthday?

Yes you do.

As the touch dissipated I looked from under the table to check on my witch. She was following Julian onto the dance floor.

Across the room I saw a hooded figure that glided toward me. I barked and barked, but no one heard me. When I looked around everyone in the room was just as they had been, but the creature had moved closer to me. As its hairy hand moved out to touch me, it suddenly pulled it back and screeched. *We will have your witch, Guardian.* The sound slithered out of its head and into mine. As it disappeared I could see the hatred in its red eyes.

A little later, I suddenly smelled food nearby and my stomach grumbled. When I peeked my head out, Jahane smiled at me. "Here, Athena. Shhhh...don't tell your mom."

I took the cheesy goodness and begged for more. Jahane loaded some on an empty plate, then placed it on the floor for me to enjoy. *Thanks.*

When Rosie and Julian came back I'd just finished the fries and licked the last bit of cheese. I plopped my head on Rosie's lap. *Mom, those were delicious. Can we have more?*

She laughed, even though I knew she hadn't heard me. I overheard Julian ask if she was ready to go home.

Bye, Jahane and Derrick. As Jahane petted me, Derrick gave me one last treat of cheesy fries. "Here ya go, girl, you were well behaved and are welcome anytime." I licked his hand and caught up to my witch.

When we arrived home, my witch and Julian disappeared into another room and I sat down in front of the box with pictures. I was bored so I clicked the remote with my paw, changing the channels.

As I lay there I sensed something and my hackles rose. I sat up and sniffed the air...it smelled like evil. Rising to my feet, a low growl emanated from me and I stalked around the room until I saw a figure out on the balcony, its cloak whipping in the wind. *What do you want*? I barked out.

The being stared at me, and I growled louder. It entered, and as it floated inside it swiped at a glass bowl on a table and knocked it over, then moved around the room. I barked louder, *Leave us,* and stood front feet apart, my head down in an attack mode.

When Rosie and Julian came running out the creature stood behind Julian, its mouth upturned in a malicious grin. I growled even louder, then crouched lower and jumped at it. As I jumped Julian barely got out of the way, but the creature disappeared in a crackling flash. I heard Rosie yell, "No!"

I ran around barking like a crazed lunatic. *Mom, there was someone here. Please, can you hear me? There was someone here.*

I heard my mom crying as she lay over Julian. My heart broke; I didn't want her sad. I shuffled sadly over to the corner of the room and tried to go to sleep.

Athena, everything will be okay; just sleep.

julian. or better yet the flea bag

hen I woke the next morning everything was quiet. I sensed Julian in the house, but Rosie was not there. I sent out a message to her but she still couldn't hear me, so I padded around the place.

Then I heard a horrible sound down the hallway that reminded me of that noisy thing that raced around on tracks. On further exploration I realized it had come from Rosie's room. I quietly walked around the corner and peered into her room and saw Julian lying in her bed...or what used to be Julian. He looked different, a little more hairy.

What in the world is going on? Where is my spirit guide when I need him?

Before I entered the room I lay on my belly. Then, as stealthily as I could muster, I crawled over to the bed. The sounds grew louder and louder the closer I approached.

I stood back up on all fours, cocked my head, and barked, then growled.

"Uh...what...?" A gravelly voice spoke.

This time my growl was louder and more menacing...or in my opinion it was.

The hairy beast man rolled over and I skidded backwards, the hair rising on my hackles. With me backed up against the wall, my barks and intermittent growls echoed around us.

"Athena, it's me," Julian crooned. "I wonder what in the world has gotten into you." He turned to me. "Hey girl, I know you don't like me, but we should become friends." His eyes turned a dark shade of red and quickly back to the color of grass.

Like hell, why don't you look at yourself in that reflection thingy? I barked at him.

He stretched and ran a hand through his hair, and the look on his face was priceless.

If dogs could smile...wait, I can.

I'd never before heard the words that flew from his mouth as he jumped up. "What in the fuck?"

Julian raised his now thickly hair covered arm and stared at it, his face looking shocked but still human. He looked down as the hair began to spread down his legs, and then looked over at me. I inclined my head toward him, backing up even further and bumping my butt into the wall, then I raised my lip and threatened him with my sharp canines.

"I won't hurt you, Athena."

Uh, yeah, sure you won't, just like those demons or hellhounds in that show Mom watches with Jahane. I could so be like those two brothers and kick your butt. I took a calculated step closer to him and felt victory when he stepped back.

I watched as the hair began to disappear and reappear, almost like it couldn't make up its mind. I stepped closer and closer, snapping my teeth. Julian glanced down at his arm and a look of confusion spread over his face. Without a second thought I lunged at him. He moved out of my way just as I snapped at him, but at the last second a bit of his shirt got caught in my teeth. He slipped out of the room and I chased him.

"Athena, I swear girl, I wouldn't hurt you," he said one last time as I stood staring at him in the doorway. Before he attempted another swipe of his hand through his hair he glanced at his arm. The hair had begun to disappear. He shook his head and it hung sadly as he walked out the door.

I promptly turned around three times and lay down, licking my paw. *I knew I could do it. I won't let a monster hurt me or Rosie. And since I'm not sure what he is, better to be safe than sorry.*

I continued licking my paw as Rosie came running through the open doorway I was protecting in case the Julian monster came back.

"Where is Julian?" she asked me.

Oh, I ran the hairy monster off. Mom, he was hairy...well, hairier than usual. I tried to get her to hear me, but all she did was pet me and continue to ask me where he was. I muttered to her, *Mom, he's gone. Hey, why don't you try dating someone else...who doesn't shed? After all, I should be the only one to shed.*

She stood up with tears in her eyes, and I felt bad for running him off. But seriously, something was wrong with this dude.

After she went in search of him I noticed a strange woman standing inside the door frame, but before I could get up Rosie came meandering back into the room. I watched as the stranger raised her hands above her head and started chanting. The woman spoke to my witch, and as she did Rosie slumped down beside me.

Mom, it will be okay, I promise. I plopped my head in her lap, hoping it would give her some sort of comfort. I felt bad for running him off, but I just couldn't help it; I seemed drawn to protect Rosie. Besides, it was my job as a Guardian.

The woman walked over to us. "You must go see the voodoo queen."

At Rosie's loud gasp I cocked my head. *Who is this voodoo queen?* After they spoke for a while the woman left.

I tried to take a nap, but my witch was pacing back and forth and her emotions were all over the place, so I couldn't. Finally she stopped. "You know, Athena? Madame Claudette is crazy...you don't go messing with voodoo."

Mom, what's this voodoo you talk about? And if it needs destroying I can kick butt. But of course she still could not hear me.

Suddenly we heard a knock on the door. My hackles rose and I growled low but steady, making the floor vibrate.

"Hush!" she told me.

When the door opened the Julian monster was standing on the doorstep. Well, just Julian, since he was no longer covered with more hair than me. I sensed an overabundance of anger pouring out from my witch. But soon it was replaced with love and compassion.

Julian sat on the sofa but I kept an eye on him. Even from my spot and with one eye closed I stayed focused on him. He shifted in the cushions and all I had to do was growl to stop him.

As I started to drift off to sleep I heard voices, then Jahane and Derrick came into the room. I stood and walked over to the burly man, and he rubbed my ears. Next I stopped beside my mom's best friend, who I adored. I sat still as she petted me, then moved over to my witch, who reached a hand over and touched me. She probably thought she was comforting me, but I thought it was the other way around.

I heard Jahane speak to Rosie and then she jumped up, and I followed. *Mom, slow down.* I ran to catch up with her. We entered our room and I crawled after her under the bed. *Mom, what are you looking for?* I sneezed when a dust bunny tried to run up my nose.

Finally we saw what we were searching for…a box. As my witch scooted out from under the bed and sat, I saw her eyes fill with water. *Mom, what's wrong?* But she wiped her face, stood up with the box in her hand, and trudged into the living room. I followed her out but felt a presence beside me. I looked up and met the kind smile of my witch's mother.

Hello, Athena, how are you and my daughter?

She's crying about something. She found a box under her bed.

Oh, dear. She shook her head and stopped.

What is it? I asked

I think she is building up the courage to tell her friends what she's been going through and her dreams. I'm also afraid she's never read my note. But that's not important right now. She leaned down and looked me in the eye. *If I know my daughter, she will try to find more. An important book that she needs is in the store. Help her find it.*

I wagged my tail and licked her, which felt funny, like dipping my tongue into water. *Yes, I'll help her.*

Before she stood back up, she ruffled my ears. *There's even something about you in the book. Now go ahead before she starts wondering where you are.*

I barked low and turned and galloped down the hall.

I skidded to a stop when I saw the items on the table, but was ushered outside with Rosie. "Come on girl, let's go to the shop."

I passed by Julian, and as he shifted positions I let out a low growl.

Hurry, Mom; we need to find a book.

I scratched on the door and finally it opened, so I pranced into the storeroom and began my search.

"How in the world are we going to find anything in here?" she asked me.

We will, I know we will. So let's get looking.

I sniffed and sniffed, my nose tracing the floor for any sign of what we were looking for. After a while, and with a lot of determination on my part to give Rosie confidence, we finally found it. As my witch picked up the box, I wagged my tail in hopes she would hurry. *I know my spirit guide, whoever it is, and Rosie's mom would be proud of me for helping Rosie.*

"Athena, this has to be the box." Excitement flowed from her through me and into the room. Her powers were becoming stronger, and in my heart I felt she would start hearing me. But I had to be patient.

As she held the box in her hand I barked in anticipation. After a search for something she called a key, we opened it. Now sitting on the ground, I wagged my tail and barked. *Hurry.*

"Ha ha. Athena, be patient."

I can't help it, Mom, this is so exciting. Please hurry, I want to see what's in the box.

As she opened the box, I stuck my nose inside and sniffed the leathery book. Rosie picked it up and a small piece of paper floated to the ground. She let the book hit the floor as she watched the paper fall. I saw tears in her eyes and shifted my attention from the book to my witch as she started to read from the small white paper. I walked over to her and placed my head on her shoulder. Glancing at the book on the floor, I nosed a few pages over. *Rosie's mom was right, there is something about me in here.*

After a few moments of silence, she stood, grabbed the book, and wiped the wetness from her face. "Come on, Athena, let's get back to the others."

My tail wagged as I ran ahead of her, crawling up the steps one at a time. The day had taken its toll on me and I was wiped.

After we entered I watched as Rosie headed into our room and came back out. I curled up in front of the door, my head on my paws, and drifted off to sleep with Karl's voice in my head.

You are doing great, Athena, I knew you would. You are gifted with magic; the tear drop amulet hanging from your collar is proof.

an old friend

he next morning in the shop I was taking my third nap of the day when I was woken by the little bell above the door. I pulled my head from the cozy place on the floor, but was too tired to get up. Besides, I didn't sense any danger from the person who came inside. Suddenly, my stomach began to growl from hunger, so I stretched my body to get all the kinks out from my nap and looked around the corner. A man walked toward my witch, but I couldn't sense any danger from him either. Rosie was staring at the door, so I thumped my tail against the counter to attract her attention to the man. *Uh, Mom, someone is here and he's talking to you.*

Well, if she wasn't going to greet him I would. After all, I thought that should be my official job title in the shop. I could see it now...Athena,

Guardian to Rosie, greeter to good people, and ripper of pants to evil people. I laughed a little, but made my way over to the nice guy with the head as shiny as one of Alisa's crystal balls.

Hi sir, how are you today? My name is Athena. My tail wagged vigorously. As the man petted me I felt a tug on my collar. *What, Mom? I was only being nice and greeting him. Besides, he is nice.*

"Stay!" she commanded me. So I skulked around the corner, whimpered, and then kept an eye on her.

After a few moments I relaxed and walked out into the courtyard. As I padded outside I saw a figure sitting in a chair by the fountain, and recognized him immediately. *Karl!* I ran full steam ahead to him and put my paws on his lap as my tail wagged in excitement. *Karl, you are here. I was so sad when you passed.*

He turned as soon as I spoke his name and my words tumbled out. His lips curved into a smile. "So, Athena, how is my favorite Guardian doing?"

I'm doing great. I stopped. *I'm your favorite Guardian, huh? Wait, are you my spirit guide?*

"Well of course. I knew you had a life destined not only to be great, but full of adventures. It will only get better, and sadly worse."

I sat back on my haunches and worried about the word "worse." *What do you mean, Karl?*

He turned to me and wrung his hands, which disappeared and reappeared as he stressed. "Yes, I am afraid it will only get worse before it gets better. An evil searches for Rosie and wishes her harm."

I growled. *I will not let them get her.*

"I know you won't. But you will have a long road ahead of you."

I sat staring at him, my tail swishing back and forth so hard it stirred up dust from the ground. *I will protect her, I promise.*

"I know you will. Now get back inside, Athena, before Rosie starts wondering where you are. Also, be nice to Julian...he's not as bad as you think."

I jumped up and licked him, and my tongue felt like it had dipped into a bowl of water. I bounced around and around before heading back inside. *See you soon, Karl.*

"Yes, we will talk later."

I stalked back inside in time to see Julian standing in the doorway. In an instant I was overcome with fear for Rosie all of a sudden and growled. The other man left and I watched, hoping he would be back soon. As I watched my witch and Julian they made odd noises and made their way upstairs. Wondering where they were going, I followed them outside, hesitantly I stopped to play in the courtyard. My eyes darted back and forth between the ghosts and the two humans walking up the steps. I ran up the steps after Rosie and Julian keeping a close eye on her, but was stopped by Magnolia. "Athena why don't you go and play Rosie needs alone time with Julian."

"Are you sure what if he hurts her?"

"He won't I promise." I hesitantly backed down the steps almost tumbling down.   but stopped to play in the courtyard.

Ghosts came out of the walls and we played a game of chase. I barked and barked. One ghost with a hat threw it, and it twirled and skidded along the stone as I tried to grab it with my teeth. As my teeth bit down it disappeared and reappeared on the ghost's head. He grinned, showing off a toothless smile. A female ghost danced around me, her skirt twirling around and around her. I nipped at the material but missed with every turn. Finally the ghosts became tired of our fun, but before returning to their hiding spots in the wall, they passed their hands swiftly over my head then darted away from me. Tired, I turned around three times before getting comfortable, and waited for Rosie to come back downstairs.

my first mardi gras parade

heard Rosie and Julian coming down the steps before I saw them. I jumped up, growled the minute I smelled Julian but when I saw Rosie I started bounding around her clearly trying to push him out of the way. *Where are we going*? My excitement grew as we headed out of the courtyard and down the street. My nose to the ground, I kept a vigilant sense on my witch.

Some people walked by us stinking of that sweet smelling scent that was found all over the place. They bumped into her, singing way more off pitch then Jahane and Julian did, and when Rosie almost fell I caught sight of Julian catching her. I heard another growl near me. *What the hell?* Looking around, I realized the growl had emanated from Julian. Not wanting to be outdone by him, my hair rose on my hackles as the group of people walked off. *Get going before I rip your pants and make you wet yourselves,* I barked after them, and stood my ground.

"OMG, are you two going to bond now?" I heard Rosie say.

But Mom, I am protecting you. I'm not sure what the Mr. Fuzzy Fleabag is doing. I bounded ahead of them after being fussed at, and up ahead I noticed Jahane. I pulled on my leash until Rosie dropped it, then ran toward Jahane. *Come on, Mom...look, it's Jahane. Hello, Jahane, how are you?*

"Athena, how are you girl?" she said as I bounced up and down around her feet.

As she petted me, I barked, *Mom will be here in a few minutes. She is with wolf boy, dog boy, or...oh, hell, he's hairier then me. Did you know that Julian has hair that covers his body like mine—well, not really like mine—Jahane?*

She never answered me, but it was just as well since my attention got interrupted when Rosie and Julian reached us. *Uh, Mom, where have you been? I've been here forever. What took you so long?*

"Bad dog," she fussed at me.

"Oh, Rosie, don't fuss at her. She couldn't help being excited to see me," Jahane told my mom. A booming voice from behind us alerted me to the burly man named Derrick. After he had hugged my mom and put her back down on the ground, I hurried up to him. He always gave the best pets. I nuzzled into his hand, accepting the comfortable touch.

The sudden loud sounds of a horn blaring had us all excited. Music that was foreign to me started thumping around me, sending vibrations though my body. I noticed my mom staring at the fortune teller lady across the street. *What's wrong, Mom?*

She grasped the amulet that she always wore around her neck. After I sensed she was okay, I ran up to Jahane to see what all the fuss was about. Tiny balls connected to each other by a string flew through the air. I jumped and twirled in the air, catching them in my mouth, flinging some around my head. Soon I was covered in a colorful assortment of the trinkets. When my mom looked over at me I wagged my tail, sending some beads flying off in different directions, thinking the whole time I was the shiz.

I turned back around to pay attention to this new experience. From down the street I saw men with skeleton masks on their faces and carrying fire on huge sticks. One removed his mask as my mom walked over to him. *Hey, it's that nice guy from earlier in the shop.* I started bouncing up and down. *Dude, I need to be petted. Hey dude, look at me, I caught a bunch of these tiny balls on a string.* But he didn't hear me...I figured it was because of all the noise surrounding us.

When Mom came back from talking to the new dude she looked agitated, but I knew it couldn't be because of him. I also noticed that the flea bag was nowhere around. *Well, good riddance*, I thought. So I trudged behind Mom, Jahane, and Derrick.

We walked into a bar that was loud with some sort of music, but not like the soulful jazz I'd grown to love here. I belly crawled on the floor and rested under the table. Realizing my fur had gotten sticky from whatever was on the floor, I knew Mom would not be happy. *Oh well, I'm too tired to worry.*

I tried to get a nap but it was hard with all the noise, so I resigned myself to watching from under the table. Two boots appeared near my spot under the table and when I peered out I saw the dude from earlier. He winked at me and I stuck my head back under the table. Finally I heard Mom get up and call to me. "Athena, let's go."

I scooted out from under the table, stopped to lick my belly, and wrinkled my nose at the taste. *I'm ready, Mom. Bye, Jahane. Bye, Derrick. Bye, new dude.*

We walked quietly down the dark street. I was on stealth mode instantly as I aimed to protect my mom. I sensed the new dude, Remi, before my mom did. *Hey look, dude, I got*

Gifted by Magic

this...no need to butt in. I can protect my mom.
He reached down and petted me and I relented.
Oh all right, you can help. But dude, I can kick ass.

He reached out to touch my mom's shoulder. It was almost funny when she jumped. "Come on, Rosie; let me walk you two home."

"Oh, all right."

I walked in between, protecting them both. When we got close to home I saw the flea bag sitting by the steps. I wanted to growl, but honestly I didn't want to make Mom upset, so I walked past him with Mom in tow. She said a few words to them both and then ushered me inside.

good things to come

 woke way before my mom and headed into the kitchen. Magically feeding myself, I was licking the last remnants from my bowl when Mom shuffled in.

Hi, Mom. Let's get going. Busy, busy day.

I followed her outside and to the shop. Once inside I started sniffing around for danger. I saw box after box, and checked them out for any danger.

"Athena, where are you?" I heard Mom calling me.

I'm in here. I pulled my head out of the box but quickly returned to my task of checking for evil in the cardboard. I heard the bell chime above the door as it opened, and I popped my head up with a necklace dangling from my nose. But my attention was diverted to the other shiny things in the box, so I plopped my nose back inside it. When I came up for air, Karl sat in a chair beside me.

So how are things going?

Karl, things are going great. I think I am getting through to her. I turned to look at him and the necklace swung. *Don't I look fabulous?*

Yes you do, Athena, he laughed.

I peeked out around the corner and saw the woman who had entered the shop. She looked familiar, but somehow I couldn't place her. My attention went back to Karl.

Athena, why don't you go ahead and see what's going on in there? Go protect your mom; something feels fishy.

All right Karl, I will. But this feeling....

It's just something in the air, Athena. I will be back...now hurry!

I bounded into the room and plopped down next to my witch's feet. A low rumble escaped me as I sat staring at this new person, whose dark hair was the color of coal...the kind cook used in the stove.

A loud squeal came from the person's mouth, and I howled at the pain it caused in my ears. From amidst the squeals I heard the word Guardian, and I cocked my head; how did this stranger know about Guardians, and me for that matter? I couldn't put my paw on it, but something was fishy, as Karl had put it.

As my witch talked to this stranger and tried to convince her there was so such thing as Guardians, I was kind of hurt, because I was so powerful. Why was she taking my existence so lightly?

Because, Athena, she is trying to protect you, Karl spoke.

I looked around but didn't see him.

The door swung open and Remi sauntered in. As soon as he walked in the stranger started making googly eyes at him.

Rosie tugged on my collar and led me to the back. I bounced up and down. *Want me to bite her? I will.* Mom started going through boxes and picked one up. *Hold on Mom, I'll help.* I walked underneath but barely touched the bottom of the box.

Athena, don't worry. You will be tall like your brother soon...it's only a matter of time. Why don't you come join me outside and let Remi help Rosie?

I saw Remi grab the box and I pranced towards the back door, opened it with my paw, and went outside where the sun was shining bright. The courtyard was full of see through people darting back and forth. One whizzed past me and I chased it, barking softly.

After a few moments of playing I saw Karl sitting by the fountain with Rosie's mom. I ambled over, sat, and looked at them.

What's going on?

43

"Hello little one...I mean Athena," Karl corrected himself and smiled. I stood and lifted my head and plopped it in his lap. The soft caress of his hand on my head made me remember my time back in Germany, and I instantly thought of Alexander.

"Athena, he is doing well. I know what you are thinking. In all my years I've never known him to get so close to any of the puppies, but you are so special in so many ways."

I looked over to Rosie's mom and noticed that she looked worried for a second before she looked at me. "Athena, you must stay close to Rosie at all times. I feel danger is close to her. It's seeking her out."

Yes, I will. I puffed my chest out and stood proud.

"Athena, she is close to truly believing in her powers and you," Magnolia said, and Karl nodded.

Really?! I sat and wagged my tail.

"Yes, she is close, so you need to push her a little more. Get into her head and make sure she hears you, and soon. As for Julian, please give him a chance. He's not as bad as you think. He has his own demons to deal with."

I swayed my head from side to side. *Okay, I'll try to give the flea bag a chance.*

She smiled and disappeared before me, leaving Karl sitting by himself.

44

"Now run inside and tend to your witch, Athena." He patted my head, stood, and vanished.

I entered just as Remi handed my mom some green paper. After he left we headed out the back door and up the steps. My witch pulled a box out of the cold box and shoved it into another big heated box, then dumped some food in my bowl.

Thanks, Mom.

She patted me and shuffled off to her room. I licked the bowl clean and added some more kibble to it. Once I was finished I waited for Rosie to return. The big heated box began to buzz and Rosie came in holding a huge book. She opened the box and pulled the contents out. I followed her to the living room as she balanced the book and the pizza, hoping she would give me a treat. *Mom, that smells good.* My belly rumbled.

She sat down and I snuggled up next to her. As she took a bite of her dinner, I sniffed. She opened the book and I felt anger surge through her. *Mom, what's wrong?* I nudged her arm. *Mom, everything will be okay.*

She began to calm and read from the book. Wondering what was in the book, I snuggled closer. "Gosh, Athena, you are getting heavier."

I'm not that heavy; now please continue to read.

She started reading about me, and I listened intently. Everything I heard was information I already knew, but it was nice to have it confirmed. She looked at me. "So Athena, are you really hundreds of years old?"

Yes, I guess I'm that old. Numbers don't really make sense to me. I know I was with Alexander for a long time, even after my brothers left to go their homes. As she continued to read I fell asleep to the sound of her voice.

I walked through the garden back in Germany. Trotting here and there, I saw Alexander and Alisa. A huge blue dog stepped out from behind a bush.

"Well hello, little sister. You've grown."

My attention diverted from the two humans, I looked into the face of my brother. "Ares! Yes, I've grown. I will soon be as big as you."

"Little sister, what's your name?"

"Athena," I replied.

"Such a great name for a powerful Guardian. I am happy you've found your witch. See, I told you it would happen. I'm so proud of you. Perhaps we will see each other again."

showing my powers

 woke to a loud sound. Turning over, I saw the book Rosie had been looking at lying on the floor. I crawled off the sofa in search of food. My dream from last night was vivid. My brother was proud of me.

Rosie woke and left me to fend for myself as she went to her room. After I'd fed myself I heard a knock on the door, so I scratched at the bedroom door.

"Hold your horses, Athena."

But Jahane is here, Mom. I bounded to the door just as Rosie opened it. In my hurry I almost knocked Jahane over. *Jahane, I've missed you.* I knew she couldn't hear me, but it didn't stop me from talking.

In that moment I decided to try something. I hadn't done this since before I'd left Germany, but what the hell? I had to get my mom's attention. I started with one ear and then the other, transforming them to stand up. I tried and tried to get the left ear to stay up, but it just flopped. Finally I sat back on my haunches and wagged my tail. My witch's face was full of shock.

Mom, I'm done with my transformation. When she stumbled back I felt elated, hoping she'd finally heard me. Her face showed it all...she *had* heard me. *Mom, you can hear me because you finally believe in yourself and me. Our powers are growing together.*

She came over to me and petted me. "You can talk to me?"

Yes, but because you were in denial you couldn't hear me until now. I guess finding that book yesterday helped you believe and stop denying.

She laughed and turned to Jahane. "Guess what? My dog is actually magical!"

Jahane stood there with her mouth hanging open. Mom popped Jahane's mouth closed as she reached for the bag she carried when we went out.

We stepped out into the bright sun. I stayed close to my mom, always keeping an eye out for danger, and sniffed a few passersby when they got too close to us. *Nope, you're not evil. But you smell like food.* The person walked off, and I continued my surveillance of the area as Rosie spoke to an old woman. Jahane and I walked over to Rosie as she finished.

"Rosie, where is the crazy woman?" Jahane asked her. I knew she was talking about that woman that had been to the house the day I'd gotten rid of Julian. I agreed with her...she was crazy, but I liked her.

"Come on, she's at her store today. Let's get going."

The trek was not long, a left here and a right there until we were finally at our destination. My paws led me into the shop behind my mom. The instant I stepped inside I got an eerie feeling. My stance told anyone who dared bother us I would do them harm.

When the air around me calmed I decided to go explore. *Mom, I'll be back. I must check out the place and make sure no evil is here.* Her thoughts were somewhere else and I knew she was safe. I could sense the protection spells around the room.

The females were chatting so I quietly went on an adventure, nosing around in every nook and cranny. I found myself behind the counter, and slipped behind the curtain of beads where Madame Claudette had come from. My senses were on high alert in this back room.

I stuck my nose in the air and smelled the strong scent of something sweet. As I sniffed some more it seemed to be dissipating. Also, the more I sniffed the air it made me light headed.

I sat down to rest a bit, plopping my head down on my paws, and saw something dangling off the table. I belly crawled over to it, and when I was a few inches from the table, I saw the most dazzling colors bounce off the walls. Two necklaces similar to my witch's were spread out on the wooden surface, their chains dangling. With my nose I gently pushed the chains back up so they wouldn't crash to the floor, taking the beautiful stones with them. I stood and placed my paws on the table. On closer inspection, I noticed one was purple and the other was green. The light from above made them sparkle even more. I wondered who they were for.

Rosie's mom shimmered in and caught me staring at the necklaces. "Those are for two special people. Now Athena, you may want to go and check on Rosie."

I looked up at her, and before I could answer her a chime sounded that pulled me from the treasure I'd found. I pranced back through the beads, stopping to bite at them as they swung back and forth, until I saw a woman who looked vaguely familiar.

Without anyone having noticed my absence, I slinked under the table close to Rosie. The woman was telling a story about the flea bag better known as Julian. The more I listened, the more intrigued I became. My senses heightened as Rosie and Jahane seemed to feel the same way I did. This Henri dude was bad news. I vowed to rip his heart out if our paths crossed.

When the story became more intense Rosie gasped. I jumped up, knocking the table slightly, and placed my head in her lap for comfort.

When the woman saw me, she gasped. "Is that a Guardian?"

Rosie gripped my collar and continued to pet me. "Yes, ma'am."

Jahane, who I guessed was overcome with excitement, interrupted the scene to ask what a Rougaroux was. I listened intently to the woman's explanation. *So that is what Julian is...some sort of wolf. No wonder he stinks sometimes.* I covered my nose with my paw.

The story told of a turn of events that made my witch cry. I saw Jahane try and comfort her, as did I. I couldn't make sense of what was going on, though I knew a slew of different emotions ran through Rosie. *Mom, it'll be okay.* But she didn't reply to me...her thoughts were all over the place, like when I chased dust bunnies in the house. Suddenly she jumped up from her seat, grabbed my leash, and ushered me outside. "Come on, Athena."

I sensed Jahane behind us, but Mom didn't stop her fast pace until Jahane stopped her. Tears streamed down my mom's face, and I didn't know what to do for her. *Mom....* She relinquished her hold on me and the three of us ambled towards the square with the huge horse statue.

argh it's pirates

fter my mom left the shop in a hurry, I trailed behind her and Jahane, keeping vigilant to be sure no one was following us. Many emotions sifted through her and I could feel each one; confusion, anger, and sadness. How could I help her? I heard the voice before I saw him.

Athena, your witch is a strong one. The way you can help her is to be there for her. Keep her close to your heart. Trust in her and yourself. The road ahead is a dangerous one.

Karl walked beside me as he spoke, but I knew I was the only one who could hear or see him. I was honored Karl had come back to lead me and help me, but somehow I knew it wouldn't last. I knew that one day I would no longer need his guidance, and I feared that day would be sooner rather than later.

I will, Karl. I stopped suddenly. *Karl, do you know that Rosie finally heard me?*

I know, little.... He quickly stopped at his familiar name for me. *We're so proud of the two of you.*

I nodded and we continued to follow the girls. We both walked in silence until we reached the square with the huge statue. I turned to Karl and he was no longer there, but his voice rang in my head. *Hurry Athena, she needs you.*

I scampered to catch up and entered the huge cast iron gates to the square. Jahane and Rosie were already sitting down on a bench. I strolled over to them and caught the middle of the conversation. Rosie's skirt slid up her leg and I saw the zig zag marks.

"But how can I have the power of healing if I can't even heal myself?" she asked.

"Because, Rosie, they only make you stronger," I heard Jahane tell her. I'd always wondered what had happened to my witch to cause such marks. My heart broke when I saw wetness slide down her face. She was doing that crying thing again.

Mom, she is right; you are so strong, I whined in her head.

She reached out to me and I placed my head in her lap. Her hand on my fur calmed us both. Then Jahane replayed the story of what happened to my Rosie so long ago. I gasped at every word. My witch had almost lost her leg to one of those creatures I met on my first day here. Instantly I wanted to stomp on one of the mules, even knowing it would probably stomp on me first. But it had hurt my Rosie.

Calm down, Athena! I heard Karl say in my head. *She holds no ill will toward them, and neither should you.*

All right, if you say so, Karl.

I turned my attention back to the conversation. The words "battle scars" made me lift my ears, and I somehow sensed they wouldn't be her last ones. But I knew the ones they spoke of had to be important ones, so I pranced around ad barked in agreement. She ruffled my fur. "Yes girl, I know I am powerful; so are you."

Jahane's excitement consumed me as she pulled Rosie up and the three of us ran off away from Jackson Square. The words "partay" and "costumes" played over and over in my head.

We crossed over what Mom called a neutral ground with soft grass surrounded by cement. It took a while...I'm not sure how long since I couldn't really tell time. I followed Jahane and Rosie into a store, and when my paws stepped inside I grew excited, though I wasn't sure why. Maybe I was feeling it from those around me.

I slinked off to see what this store contained. It was so different than the one we owned. Over by the back wall I found some boxes and began nosing though them. The items were nothing like I'd seen or felt before. They were soft, feathery, hard, and scratchy. I grabbed a few things with my teeth, careful not to tear or break anything. I threw the feathery thing over my shoulder, since the feathers kept getting stuck in my teeth and on my tongue. After I was satisfied with my loot I pranced back over to Rosie. *Look what I found, Mom.*

She doubled over with laughter as she took the mask I had dangling from my mouth by the string.

Duh, Momma, it's my costume.

"Well, you'll definitely fit in with us." She laughed again.

I know, that's why I picked it out. Duh. But she never heard me, I guessed, because she was busy giving the man at the counter some green paper.

I trailed a few feet away from them, listening and sniffing for danger. *Athena, it looks as if you are growing into a new power. Can you sense what Rosie will do as she is doing it or before she does it?* Karl asked, reappearing beside me.

I guess so. I mean, I knew they were picking out pirate costumes even though I am not sure what a pirate is, but I sensed a parrot was needed to go along.

He laughed silently. *You amaze me every day. You are becoming a telepath. There was only one other Guardian with that power.*

I stopped. *Who?*

Your mother. Before Alexander even created the Guardians and Warriors, your mother had special abilities that he used in the potions he gave you and your brothers. But she was not created from a potion...she had it to enhance her abilities. She was magical already, though we are not entirely sure of how that came to be. My family, who were Roma gypsies, gave your mom to Alexander to protect his wife. Little did we know she would be the first of a very important line.

I noticed Jahane and Rosie had stepped inside another store and I waited for them to come out. *Karl, how did you know my mother, or dog mother, was magical?*

Well, the day that the witches and warlocks came to Alexander asking for help, a war against the magical community was raging. The townsfolk were scared of things they had no understanding of. Witches were being burned due to the clash of religions in that time. I'd sent Alexander to my family. There had been a prophecy that the witches would be hunted down, so he got a Great Dane for his wife Dahlia for protection. They bonded instantly. It was as if they would have secret conversations with each other.

The day they came and took Dahlia, they also took your mother. I heard the scream in my head as well. Persephone was barking madly, biting, snarling, growling. I could understand

56

her somewhat, though I hadn't mastered my powers yet...I was still young. But I knew that Dahlia had screamed for Persephone to come help her. They locked Persephone away but she was able to escape. I knew those two could communicate and Persephone would find her. The next day Alexander and I went to the courts, but they had condemned Dahlia to death. As the flames burned, Persephone pulled Dahlia out of the fire and was lying next to her. They were conversing to each other and only each other. They had somehow found a way to block others with powers like mine from hearing them.

Before I could ask him a question, Rosie and Jahane came out of the store. "Come, Athena."

I'll finish my story another time, Karl said as he nodded at me and disappeared. I wanted to make him finish, but the smell that came from whatever Rosie was carrying had my full attention.

Once at home I couldn't help but wonder what we were going to be doing that night. Everyone was excited; even Julian and Derrick arrived. I didn't get the creepy factor from Julian like I usually did.

While I waited for the humans to get dressed, I grabbed my stuff in my mouth and trudged off down the hall. The mask dangled from my mouth and the feathers from the boa got stuck on my tongue, and I coughed and hacked up a few wet feathers. I let the mask fall out of my mouth, but the string caught on my bottom right canine.

The smell of lavender and magnolias floated through the room. Before I could remove the mask, a hand reached out and slipped it from my tooth. *Athena, take care of my Petal tonight.*

I bobbed my head and my ears stood up straight. *Yes, I'll do my job perfectly.*

Good girl. Rosie's mom smiled down at me. She knelt down and while our faces were inches from each other, I could see sadness reflected in her eyes. She rubbed my head and I leaned into her touch, which was so similar to Rosie's.

Magnolia stood and turned away from me. I glanced down at the mask and willed it to land on my face, and she turned back and laughed. *Athena, you make the most amazing parrot*

I pulled my jowls back in a smile. *Thank you.* The boa flew around my withers and wrapped around my neck. *I'll protect her with my life.*

Good! She turned and disappeared.

I ran off down the hall with feathers flying behind me. As soon as I skidded to a stop in front of the merry band of pirates Derrick busted out laughing. I pranced around at his evident approval of my costume. *I picked it out all by myself*, I barked out.

Before we left I sat back as my merry band of pirates raised glasses to each other. My nose sniffed the most delicious aroma, so I stood and walked over to the kitchen. There it sat, all different colors and doughy. I looked around at the humans; no one was paying attention, so I reached up and gently took a piece of the cut cake. *Mmmm.* The sweetness slid down my gullet, and the middle was filled with creaminess. *Mom, what is this*? I asked as I licked the sugary bits off my nose. She never heard me...not because she couldn't, but because she was too much in the moment. I reminded myself to ask her later. As they were all talking, I snuck another piece for later, putting into my metal bowl.

Finally we headed out, my nose to the ground. The smells were the same as ever...the revolting smell of different alcohols permeated the uneven cobblestone sidewalks. Every once in a while I caught a whiff of the sweet smell of urine, each odor as unique as its owner.

Even though I sniffed as I walked, my ears were alert to my surroundings. I was attuned to everything. I weaved in and out of the thick crowd, careful to not get stepped on or get the yucky alcohol spilled on my coat.

As I followed my humans, someone stepped in front of me, blocking my path. Every step I took, the drunk human matched. I was beginning to get annoyed. After a few moments of this dance, I finally nipped the intoxicated guy in the crotch with my incisors. He yelped, and held himself there but moved out of my way so I could continue with my party.

When I reached my group, I noticed Rosie standing as still as a statue. *Mom, what's...?* I stopped when I saw the creature. It oozed evil. The only thing I knew to do was stand as close as I could to her. I felt my magic envelope the both of us as the creature spoke to her. I leaned in closer. *Mom, we got this.*

She never answered, just held her amulet in her hand. I turned to the monster and growled. *You will never have her powers.* He or it ignored me. I blinked and the creature was gone.

Jahane came up next to us. "What was that?" she asked.

Yeah, Mom, what was that? I brushed up against her.

"It can't be real...it was an old folktale come to life. But let's discuss this later."

I cocked my head at her, and felt Karl's presence before I saw him. *Athena, be careful. You witnessed the evil that is after Rosie.*

My head whipped around as he knelt down beside me. *I knew it was evil...it smelled.*

He patted me on the head. *Athena, be careful, but protect Rosie; it's your job.*

I will, Karl.

He stood and laughed as he glanced at the crowd. *Are you enjoying yourself in this place?*

He grinned as I bobbed my parrot head. *Yes Karl, I am. They have the most delicious food...and look at me.* I danced around, letting my boa blow in the wind. *I am a parrot.*

He laughed even harder. *I wish Alexander could see you now. You seem to have become more confident and are becoming a fine Guardian. Remember though, you are to protect.*

I stopped dancing. *Yes, I will remember. I think Rosie needed this, though. She is so stressed, but look at her...she is having fun! Though I am still not sure about Julian, first and foremost, I protect.*

He patted me on the head before he disappeared. *Go have fun with your witch.*

I ran off in her direction and saw Rosie talking to a new person, one with red hair like Alexander's.

My humans bounced from place to place. They drank that horrid alcohol and I kept an eye out for them, even Julian. After hours and hours of partying, though, I could tell Rosie was getting tired.

"Bye guys...it's getting late. I'll see y'all tomorrow." I watched as she told her friends goodbye. My paws pranced down the cobblestone street, and the place smelled even worse than before. Balls on strings, plastic cups, and uneaten food littered the road. I sidestepped someone's vomit. The sun was coming up as I followed her and Julian home.

hot dogs and clean up

olling over in bed, my jowls flopping back, I stretched a bit, feeling for my mom. I looked around and saw I was the only one in bed. *Mom!* I called out. I stretched a bit more then stood up in the bed. With no sign of her I jumped out of bed and headed out to the kitchen. Still no sign of her. *Oh well, I'll get a bite to eat before searching for her.*

I looked in my bowl and the piece of cake I had placed there called out to me. My stomach growled, so I stalked over, guarding my cake. Taking the whole piece in my mouth, I discovered that the outside was a little hard this morning. At first my tongue licked the sugary icing off, then my teeth dug into the soft cake. But the ooey gooey was still a little creamy. I needed to remember this dessert for another time...maybe Mom would get me more.

After breakfast I hurried outside, opening the door with my paw. The sun was bright, and I blinked as I took the steps down and into the courtyard. As I walked around I saw Remi; or as Jahane called him, hot brown love. I barked loudly.

Remi turned to me "Hey girl, how ya doing?"

I'm doing well, I barked out, knowing he couldn't understand me.

He petted me on the head and scratched behind my ears. This man was so nice to me. After he stopped I sat back and looked at what he was doing. "So Athena, want to help me today?"

Sure, I barked. I wasn't sure how I could help him, but was willing to try.

He stood and grabbed another piece of wood. "Come girl, help me lift this."

I pranced over and nudged the board with my nose, grabbed the edge in my mouth, and lifted. We both carried it over to the other pieces. "Good girl. Thanks. You sure are strong for your size, though I'm sure you are going to get bigger."

You are welcome, I barked out.

I saw Rosie come out from the store and the look on her face was comical...almost the same look she gave Julian. She quickly composed herself.

Remi smiled at her. "I am almost done here."

"Okay, Remi. I need to step out for a bit. Satan's bitch is here and wants to talk to me."

"You really don't like her, do you?" he asked.

Wait Mom, I'll go with you.

I vaguely heard Remi speaking to her.

"Lock up when you are done. Come on, Athena. Let's go."

I bounded over to her and licked her face. *Sure, come on, let's go.* I wiggled as she clipped on my leash.

I pranced inside and saw a woman in the store...the one from the other day who had upset Mom. A wave of familiarity hit me, but I wasn't sure how I knew this woman. There was an odd aura surrounding her. I shook it off, determined to look into it further. Maybe I would ask Karl.

I sat staring at the two, trying to will my ears up, but only one still stood. Concentration had me sticking my tongue out. My mom laughed at me. "Come on, let's go." Then the other ear dropped back down.

I stood and followed them out the door.

The sun was warm on my fur as we rounded the corner to the big square. Up ahead I saw the man who had given me my first treat when I arrived here. *Hello*, I barked out, remembering him from my first day.

"Hello, puppy," the toothless man spoke.

Do you have any more of those treats? I sat and wagged my tail. About that time my mom and the woman walked up.

"Hello, Miss Rosie," I heard the man tell my mom.

"Hello. Raoul. Can we have three lucky dogs?"

"Sure thing, Miss Rosie."

The smell of the treats wafted to my nose as he dipped them out of the huge hotdog shaped cart. My tail swished back and forth in anticipation, and my mouth watered. When Raoul handed me my treat I gently took it from him. *Thanks, Raoul,* I barked out the side of the mouth, careful not to drop my hotdog.

I followed my mom with my hotdog in my mouth and sat down beside her. Placing it on the ground, I started to eat. In two bites I gulped it down and then licked my lips...I wanted more. I looked up and saw Raoul grinning at me. I gazed up to my mom and she was in deep conversation with the woman called Gabby, so I trotted off over to the hotdog man. He was waiting for me with a treat in his stubby fat hand. He held the hot dog out to me and I grabbed it. "Hello again, puppy."

Hello, Raoul, I barked. This time I took no time and scarfed the bread and meat down, and felt it slide down my throat. Then I sat down and gazed up at him again.

"You want another one?"

I nodded at him and he turned and dipped another one out and handed it to me. I gobbled it up. *Thank you,* I barked out.

He petted my head. "Come back anytime, pup, and I'll have hot dogs for you," he laughed with a toothless grin.

I barked and ran back over to my mom. Once back I found a nice warm spot on the cobblestone street beside the black iron bench.

All of a sudden I heard Jahane's voice. I stood and a smell wafted to me. The smell was coming from my paw, so I picked it up and licked it. *Yum, left over hot dog.*

After licking my paw I lumbered over to Jahane, and my head played tennis as I watched the looks they gave Gabby, who I felt in my bones was off somehow. The waves of distrust coming from my witch like a storm made me want to investigate this more. But a funny feeling ebbed around me and I looked up at Gabby, who just returned my gaze with a smile. I shook my head and my ears flopped against my head. Jahane, Rosie, and Gabby began walking towards Miss Alina's so I followed, my leash dragging against the ground.

Upon entering, the smell of fresh baked cookies hit my nose, and I lifted it in the air and sniffed. My mouth salivated and I drooled. "Athena, here ya go, girl." Rosie tossed a cookie and I jumped midair and caught the delicious morsel. Plopping down on my belly, I rested my head on my paws and watched the interaction of the humans in the room. Uneasy feelings surged through the room, but I shook my head. "Athena, come on, girl," I heard Rosie call to me.

I jumped up, stretched, and followed her to a back room. Once in the back I climbed up on the sofa and made myself comfortable, hanging my head off the cushion. A smell of sweet flowers and lavender circled around me and comforted me. I yawned and stretched out more on the sofa. Miss Alina reached out and scratched my ears, and I kicked out a leg at the touch. *Geez, that felt good.*

"You, Athena, are growing quite well," Alina commented.

My head popped up and I barked in agreement. After a few more minutes I stood, jumped off the sofa, and went to explore to give them a chance to talk. I knew my mom missed her mom, and Alina was the closest thing to her she could get.

My paws carried me to another back room filled with the most delightful sights, toys, and oh my, more toys. I ran into the room and skidded to a halt in front of squeaky toys and stuffed toys. My mouth salivated at all the awesomeness in this room. I plopped down in the middle off all this fun, squeaking my way through plastic treat after another. Tearing apart a stuffed bear, I growled at his torn apart body. Well frankly because its beady little eyes stared at me, begging for me to rip them out.

As I sat amongst all my destruction I heard laughter. My head popped up and I looked up to see Karl. Fur and stuffing dangled from my canines. *What?* I asked through the spit covered fluff. I spat out the round squeaky bits and stuffing, but not before getting one last squeak from it.

Karl laughed loudly. "Don't you think Miss Alina will be a little upset at this destruction?" He waved an opaque hand at what I'd done.

I stood and shook off some dead toy remnants from my fur. It rippled as the fluff, stuffing, material, and hard objects all flew in the air and landed on the floor. I stepped over all the dead toys and looked back at what I'd done. *Oh no, I'm going to be in deep trouble*, I whined.

He laughed again. "I doubt it; you know you can fix it."

I can?

"Yes, Athena, you can."

But how?

"Concentrate on the mess, and then concentrate on fixing it."

I stood, spread my legs out, and stared down at the mess I'd made. Fixating my mind on the mess in the middle of the room, I concentrated hard. Fluff, stuffing, squeakers, and colored material all lifted in the air, but quickly fell back to the floor.

"Try again, Athena." I did as he instructed. Shock rolled off me and I almost lost my concentration until I heard a distant voice behind me. "You can do it, little one."

My body stood a little taller as confidence reigned around me. The air was filled with bits of fluff flying here and there, trying to find where it belonged. After the third time, stuffing, fur, and squeakers floated in the air, and piece by piece each toy was magically fixed. Before my eyes all the toys were once again whole. I popped the last glass eyeball into a stuffed raccoon and then dropped all the toys back on the ground as if they'd never been disturbed. My tongue hung from the corner of my mouth and I sighed after repairing all the damage.

"Little one, you did it!" His use of my old nickname hit home for me.

I turned my head and grinned. *I did do it.* I bounced around his feet and came to rest as the excitement dissipated a bit.

"Athena, I think it's time you return to the other room. I'm so proud of you. Alexander would be proud of you, too."

You think so? Because I sure hope. I leaned up, placed my paws on his knees, and licked him in the face. Turning on my heels, my tail hit him in the face as I headed back to the room where Rosie and Miss Alina were.

I rounded the corner in time to see tears roll down my witch's face. The mention of her mother visiting us at the castle caught my ears, and I scuffled in and sat beside her. She was showing a mark on her body.

My chest burned a smidge and I nudged Rosie with my head. *Mom, I have one too.* I pushed my chest into her view, revealing my mark. She touched it and heat bubbled around my body, infusing into every part of me. A variety of colors spread through my fur and leaped from me to Rosie, to the tear drop on her hip. *What does this mean?* I wondered.

A voice spoke in my head. *Guardian, you are now bonded forever with my daughter in more than one way.* My fur rippled along my body as the faint smell of a sweet flower invaded my nose. I sat patiently, waiting to leave.

Rosie, we are bonded forever now.

I know, Athena; isn't it great? She spoke to only me through our magical gifts.

We entered the front room and Jahane jumped up from her chair. "Are y'all ready to go?"

Rosie nodded. "Let's go."

I followed both outside into the beautiful day, knowing everything I had gone through to get here was worth it.

marie laveau and ghosts

he three of us walked into the apartment and I immediately went to the box with moving pictures and turned it on. The sound blared and I jumped. Turning it down with my mind, I got comfortable on my belly. My eyes scanned the show, but I became bored and fell fast asleep. The dreams that plagued me were scary.

Darkness smothered me. I tried with all my might to untangle myself from the evil. "Athena, follow me out of the darkness." I did as the voice asked of me. The gravel walkway crunched underneath my paws, but I stopped to sniff the ground. "Hurry!" the voice prodded me, so I continued on my way.

The leaves in the trees began to blow, fluttering to the ground from their perch on the branches above me. My steps quickened as the leaves fell faster. My nose sniffed the air and the smell of burnt sulfur suffocated me. I fell to the ground. Evil surrounded me still.

From the fog I found myself inching on my belly to the light ahead. "Athena." The voice prodded me closer. As I crawled away from the darkness I still didn't understand what was happening to me.

In the distance I saw a woman sitting on a tree stump. The closer I got, the slower I stalked. "Athena, don't be frightened of me."

I stopped and sat mere inches from her, and cocked my head. This woman was not familiar to me, but her face showed kindness. "Athena, my name is Marie Laveau."

I scooted closer to her, relishing in her comfortable, soothing voice. "What is happening to me?" I barked out.

"I've entered your dream; it is one of my many talents. I wanted to see the Guardian who belongs to Rosie." She picked up my paw and examined it, then her gaze scanned over my rose mark on my chest. I puffed it out, feeling proud of the mark. "You are a fine Guardian. Alexander did great—"

"You know Alexander?" I interrupted her.

"Pup, I know lots of things...some you would never imagine."

I was intrigued, but before I could ask more questions I was pulled from my dream. A voice rang in my head. "Protect Rosie; she will need it. Now hurry and go to her."

On the cold floor I stretched my body then popped open my eyes. Jahane and my witch were sitting there among an assortment of items. They stood and I followed suit, nudging the door open with my mind. At my look of "Come on let's go," they both started laughing.

"Damn, Rosie, can we get her to get drinks from the fridge?"

I ambled over to the cold box, opened it, and grabbed two brown bottles from it. With the items in my mouth I trudged back over and stood, then sat thumping my tail back and forth on the floor. *Here, Mom.*

"Geez, Athena."

What Mom?

"Are you trying to drive Jahane crazy and send her to the looney bin?"

No Mom, but I thought she wanted a drink. I wagged my tail, still holding onto the bottles.

She took one and wiped my treasurable drool off or that's how I looked at the wetness I'd lavished on her. Jahane stood there with her mouth hanging open, so I nudged her with my head, offering her the other bottle. She took it and laughed.

My paws hit the wooden slats of the steps as we descended into the courtyard. From the corner of my eye I saw a fleeting figure floating around. I watched it toy with me and decided to stay and play after I watched Rosie and Jahane walk into the shop.

Once they were safe inside I crouched down low as the ghost flitted back and forth around me. My butt up in the air, I shook to the left then to the right. Waiting for the right moment, I pounced the moment the see through person got close to me, but my teeth went right through it. Pulling back, I muttered, *Damn, almost.*

The ghost grinned and flew back toward me, then materialized before me. "Hello, pup."

I sat down, leaned in, and sniffed him, but my nose went right through him. He sat down on the ledge around the fountain and reached out to ruffle my ears. "So you are the little pup for whom my boss requested me to send playmates your way."

With my head held up I looked at him. *Who are you?*

"Oh dear, where are my manners? My name is Markos. I'm in charge of all ghosts that come into the city, and I find them jobs."

It's nice to meet you. I offered my paw to him; he chuckled low and shook it.

"And your name is?"

I stood and puffed out my chest. *My name is Athena.*

"It's nice to meet you, Athena. I have it on good authority you are an important pup. We have been given strict orders to watch over you. We will always be here for you if you need us."

There are more of you?

He laughed. "Oh, you are in New Orleans, the center of paranormal activity."

Relaxing, I sat back and my curiosity held my attention on this ghost. *What do you mean?*

Before he could answer, a few dozen ghosts emerged from the walls, followed by Karl. They floated above me, waving to me. Markos and Karl nodded to each other as Karl walked over to me. "He means, Athena, that New Orleans is well known for its ghosts, witches, vampires, and other unexplainable things. You are actually one of those as well. Magic is all around us, whether in the form of ghosts or witches, or Guardians." He winked at me.

My eyes looked up and I scanned a few dozen wisps of people smiling down at me. They were all dressed differently...some looked really old, some young.

A young woman about the age of my witch floated down, her green eyes kind as she looked in my direction. "Markos, we must get going. It's almost dark, and I want to mess with the tourists before work."

"Sure, Esmerie, I'm coming. Bye, Athena. If you ever need someone to play with let us know. There will always be someone here."

I nudged his hand. *Bye, ghost friends.* My body swiveled back to face Karl. *Now what?*

He laughed. "Now you go see what your witch is up to. It looks like her friends have a surprise for her."

Sure enough, Julian, Remi, and Derrick were headed into the store carrying a huge wooden thing. *Bye Karl.* My voice carried over to him as I followed the men into the shop.

We entered and Rosie squealed at her surprise. I was not sure what all the excitement was about. It wasn't like it was a giant cookie, or a toy, or even a frog for that matter.

My thoughts were interrupted. "Hey, who is in the mood for pizza?" I heard Derrick's gruff voice ask.

Pizza! I barked out. *Me me me.* I danced around, my mouth salivating at the mention of food. The guys left to go get my dinner and I sat beside Rosie.

As the excitement settled I curled up and waited for the guys to come back with pizza. The scent of cheese and pepperoni wafted through the air even before the guys walked in. I jumped up and wagged my tail.

The moment the box was placed on the table I sniffed it. I couldn't wait any longer...my stomach growled in anticipation. As the humans chatted, I opened the box and stealthily slid a piece out.

Slinking off to a hiding spot, the triangle treat dangled from my mouth. I curled up on the floor and dug in. *The cheese! OMG, the ooey gooey cheese!* I licked my lips as the last string of cheese hit my tongue.

The humans were having fun, but I grew tired. I grabbed another piece and headed off to the apartment. Being extra careful not to drop my slice, I made it up the steps.

The apartment was dark when I entered, so I turned on the lights. The door to the fridge opened and I was amazed at how my powers were growing. Since exhaustion was taking over, I gently placed my pizza slice on the shelf. I would save it for later. The door closed to the cold box and I trotted off to the bedroom.

The blanket on the bed called to me, and my eyes grew heavy as I crawled into bed. Turning around three times, I finally got comfortable and fell fast asleep.

All of a sudden I was jerked from my deep sleep. "Athena, get out of bed."

I popped one eye open to see Rosie in the flea bag's arms. She looked tired, so I blinked, stood slowly, stretched, and then finally jumped out of bed. *Geeze, Mom, you didn't have to yell.* I sulked out of the room, found a new spot, and curled up, and within seconds was sound asleep again.

the flea bag's conundrum

stirred and my belly growled, so I popped one eye open and glanced around. I knew my mom was not up since the sounds of snoring bounced off the walls. Goodness, she was loud. I rolled over and stretched a bit, then stood, stretching a bit more. All that was necessary now was to fill my belly with food.

Padding over to the cold box, I opened it with my nose and dug around until I found my piece of pizza. I closed the door and sat down, protecting my food from anyone who might dare try to take it. My first bite was heavenly as I held onto the end with my paw and bit into it. A long string of cheese pulled as I ate. I felt my eyes roll back in my head as I finished the last morsel.

Footsteps shuffled down the hall and I turned around and growled. The flea bag stopped dead in his tracks as he rounded the corner. "What's wrong, girl?" he cooed at me.

In no way at all was I falling for his tricks. He slowly stepped towards me and I backed up, tasting a bit of cheese on my lip. My tongue popped out and licked it.

Julian made his way into the kitchen, keeping an eye on me. After a while, I smelled scrumptious smells wafting through the room. Hesitantly I stalked into the room and peeked around the door. Julian smiled down at me.

"Hey girl, want a bite of egg?"

I tilted my head and stared at him as he tossed a bit of yellow food at me. I sniffed it, not really wanting to take it from the flea bag.

"Oh, come on, Athena," he begged.

My mouth salivated as the intoxicating smell called out to me to eat it. I sniffed it one more time, then scooped it up off the floor. *Wow, this is actually good.*

He smiled. "See girl, we can be friends."

Not until you get rid of your fleas. I huffed off into the living room to watch TV. I barely heard him leave the kitchen, humming as he left, I guessed, to go and check on my witch.

A while later I heard them coming down the hall, so I quickly turned the TV off and grabbed my leash. After Rosie clipped my leash to my collar I opened the door. My head whipped around to tell them to hurry, and Julian was staring at me. Before I could ask Rosie if Julian didn't realize I was magical, she grinned at him. "I'll tell you later."

Oh wow, if he knew what I was, he would totally freak. This might be funny, I barked as we left and I shut the door with my mind.

The mood was solemn as the three of us walked down the street. Because I sensed that Rosie's guard was down from worry about the flea bag, I was on high alert for all of us.

Everyone's emotions were on overload as we approached Madame Claudette's shop. Finally we stepped inside, and I saw that the lady with the hair as red as Alexander's was there. But then I remembered this place was hers. She waved my witch and Julian over to sit down. I sat beside Rosie, then crawled under the table when I saw a piece of cookie underneath. My nose sniffed at it. *Yum, chocolate chip*! Quickly I slurped it up, crunched it, and swallowed.

As I moved back out from underneath the table I saw Karl over in the corner of the room. As I zoomed over to him, I noticed his face was serious. *What's wrong, Karl?*

Athena, pay close attention to what they discuss today.

I nodded, sauntered back over to the table, and focused my attention on the humans sitting around the table.

The mood was somber and I could feel the tension in the room, and I could almost taste the stiffness. My body instinctively leaned closer to Rosie as the story was told.

"Julian, how much of your family history do you know?" I heard the woman ask him.

"Not much."

As his story unfolded I noticed that Julian seemed different, almost sad. But after hearing the tale—how and why he was cursed—for myself, I felt for him. I desperately wanted to understand what a Rougaroux was. It had to be some sort of creature that had fleas.

Some more talking took place, and then our attention shifted to Julian's rising anger and his chair falling over backwards.

I growled. *Don't hurt my Rosie.*

Alina reached out a hand and petted me. It calmed me a little, but now I was on high alert. The presence of Karl standing beside me settled me some more. *Athena, this is not his fault. He has been cursed. In fact, it is a curse that is detrimental to him. You may want to give him a second chance.*

My head whipped around, almost bumping into the table. *What do you mean?*

He knelt down beside me. *Marie Laveau cursed Julian's family; this is not his fault.*

Is that why he is different, why he gets angry and gets more fleas than I do?

He chuckled slightly. *Yes, but more importantly, he will need both you and Rosie if he is to beat this curse. He and Rosie have a long road to travel, and it will not be an easy one.*

He will need me too?

Yes. You are Rosie's Guardian, and since he will need her more than ever, he will need you as well.

With a sigh, I padded over to Julian and nudged his hand. *I understand this is not your fault,* I told him, knowing he couldn't hear me, but Rosie could.

He leaned down to my level. "Hey girl, so you don't hate me after all, huh?" He reached a steady hand out and petted my ears. I leaned into the touch.

No, I don't hate you, but you better not hurt my Rosie. With that I stuck my tongue out and dragged it down his face, finding some satisfaction in his taste.

He laughed loudly and wiped the drool off.

Hey, that was good drool, dude.

Karl stood beside me. *Good job, Athena. Now that you know what is wrong with him, you can protect them both...though Rosie is your first priority.*

I stood and leaned into Rosie and gazed at the humans. Rosie leaned back into me and said, "I swear, you will never cease to amaze me."

My job is to protect you, and I will with my life.

I watched as she headed off to the back with the strange lady. Julian sat slumped in a chair, so I nudged him with my head. He absentmindedly petted my head. At his touch his pain ebbed through my body. "Thank you, Athena." His voice was almost inaudible.

I barked and leaned my body closer to him, hoping to comfort him some more.

Rosie came out from the back and Julian stood and grabbed her hand. "Are you ready to go, cher?"

She nodded and the three of us left the shop.

visit to see the voodoo queen interrupted

he next morning I left Rosie and Julian alone. They were going through something, but I was still on alert in case they needed anything. I trudged into the kitchen and kibble found its way magically into my bowl. My belly growled and I dug in.

A see through person flew through the walls, and as it did it waved for me to follow. Quickly I finished my food and headed outside and down the steps into the bright light of my playground. Ghostly apparitions danced in the sunlight as I galloped down the steps, the hard wood pressing into my paws. I skidded to a stop at the edge and watched the show.

Karl sat on the edge of the fountain and watched as well. I danced up to him and placed my head in his lap. The balancing act I'd become used to when I touched him was getting easier and easier.

While I was careful not to let my head go through his lap, he turned to me and placed his hand on my head. The comfort of his touch sent me back to my time in Germany. I missed my brothers, but I knew they had good lives, as did I.

"So Athena, how are you this morning?"

I'm okay, though I know Rosie and Julian are going through things. The thoughts in their heads make me sad.

His hands slowed their movement on my head. "I know, but with your help they will figure things out."

What can I do?

"The only thing you can do. Be there for them both."

How?

"By helping Rosie and protecting her. With your love and help she will be confident in the decisions she must make. Especially with the battle she will be faced with."

Karl, what must she decide?

"Well, she must speak to the voodoo queen Marie Laveau in order to help Julian."

The voodoo queen?

"Yes, little Guardian. She is the one who has placed this curse on his family."

But if she cursed his family, why would she help Rosie?

"Because your witch is powerful and her mother was friends with Marie Laveau. Though Rosie must be careful; the voodoo queen is not an evil entity, but she is not one to trifle with." I angled my head and looked up at him. He ruffled my ears. "Be ready for anything, and always stay alert. Rosie will need you in the coming months."

Within a blink of an eye he disappeared, and me and the still dancing ghosts were all that was left. They waved for me to join them, but my thoughts were elsewhere. The see through people sadly took their leave, disappearing back into the walls of the courtyard. I trudged slowly back up the steps, but felt a presence beside me. When I looked over I saw a ghostly figure. It mouthed, *Don't worry, pup, you can do this,* then smiled a three toothed grin and vanished.

A few nights later Rosie came shuffling out of the bedroom and put a metal thing on the food maker. She was quiet, but stirred when it made a whistling noise. Her thoughts were all over the place. I could feel her emotions through my body.

"Athena, we must go see the voodoo queen."

I know, Mom. I scooped up her shoes in my mouth and walked over to her. She smiled weakly at me and took my offering. I knew she was battling a decision, but I would be there to help her. *Come on, Mom, let's go.*

"Do you think we are ready for this?" she asked.

I barked.

"Okay, let's get going before Julian wakes up."

Quietly we slipped outside. The ghosts in the courtyard were cheering us on as we made our way out. *You've got this. Protect the witch.*

I sensed Rosie was spooked by her tight grip on my leash as we headed down the streets. We hastened our steps, and my ears perked at noises in the shadows. I felt Rosie's anxiety hit high.

"Who's out there?" No one answered, so we continued down the cobblestone sidewalk.

I remained on high alert. *Mom, it will be okay.* I leaned into her body as she walked.

"I know, Athena." She sidestepped a bag of garbage but caught herself.

Evil laughter erupted around us. I looked around and saw a hooded figure in the distance, its red eyes staring back at me. It opened its mouth to reveal sharp teeth inside. I heard it talking but I knew it wasn't directed to me.

"Hurt her now!"

The words seethed out of his mouth. I thought, *Hurt who, my Rosie? Mom, Mom, watch out!* I tried to get my mom's attention, but she was distracted.

As she turned the corner, she bounced off something big. My hackles instantly rose against my spine. A huge animal stood before us, something I'd never seen before. I growled and pushed my jowls back over my canines. *If you do anything to my mom, I'll rip your throat out.* The creature never acknowledged me.

Through all the noise I heard Rosie's pleas. "Athena, come here!" I backed up towards her, never stopping my growl, though it got louder and bounced off the blowing wind. I felt her hand the moment it touched me. I hoped to calm her.

The creature, though, was not heeding my warnings. It stalked Rosie menacingly as she moved backwards. Rosie fell as she tried to get away and glanced at her hand. The smell of blood hit my nose and I knew she was hurt.

I growled even louder as the creature touched her. I looked behind him and saw the hooded figure pushing him even further to hurt my Rosie. "Do it!" the evil kept saying.

A light brightened the whole street and the figure vanished before me. I looked up to see one of the woman from the fortune teller's shop walking down the street, light encasing her. The creature looked at her then to us before it backed away from us and ran off.

The woman came up to us. "Are you okay, Rosie?"

Rosie didn't answer, just drew herself into a tight ball.

"Child, we must get you back home."

I barked in agreement. *We need to go home, Mom.*

Rosie looked up. "How did you know I was here? Why do you have lights coming from your hands?"

"That we can discuss later."

"I need to get the cemetery...I need to help Julian."

"No, not tonight. My ancestor can wait." She shook her head and I saw confusion in her expression. "If he has made the complete change it means another evil is here. But he must have killed someone in order to turn, or...damn," she cursed under her breath. "We must get you home."

As the woman helped my mom up I looked over to the empty street and saw the hooded figure standing there. Its robe blew in the wind as it mouthed, *You are next, Guardian.*

I barked at it and turned to follow my witch home.

Back at home, Rosie's emotions were all of sadness. She curled up in the bed, so I jumped up and lay at the foot. "Athena you take care of you witch, evil is in the Quarter. You must be careful." The lady who'd rescued my mom said. As we drifted off to sleep I heard soft sobs from my witch.

heartbreak marie laveau and baron samedi oh my

he next morning I paced, waiting anxiously for Rosie to answer the door. My senses were on high alert, and I sensed Julian outside. Rosie opened the door and the flea bag looked horrible. "Come on in, Julian," I heard Rosie tell him. He was not his usual self, but more subdued.

Rosie poured some food into my metal bowl, so I slinked into the kitchen and munched on it. The sense that something was wrong settled deep in my belly.

After I ate the last morsel I saw Karl over in the corner. *Athena, Rosie will need you more than ever in a few minutes.*

I looked up and licked my lips, the taste of beef remaining. *Why? What is going to happen?*

Watch, little one.

The familiar nickname brought my head up to view the sight before me. My heart broke at what I witnessed. Rosie's tears streamed down her face as she begged Julian to stay, but he turned to walk out the door. He looked at me and mouthed, *Take care of her, Athena. This is for her protection.*

"No, Julian, don't leave me!" I heard her scream."

I saw the pain on his face as he turned and looked at Rosie one more time before leaving.

Athena, he is afraid he will hurt her. He's doing this to protect her.

Are you sure? Confusion surrounded me.

Yes. Besides, he has his own journey to go through.

Pain filled every fiber of me as I felt Rosie's heartbreak. I heard a loud crash and watched as the thing she talked on broke into small pieces. My body shook uncontrollably from the pain she was experiencing.

Mom, it will be all right. I ran over to her as she lay heaving on the floor. My body covered her, but she never moved except for the few times she woke and began to cry again.

After what seemed like hours, I heard voices at the door and picked up my head. Derrick and Jahane stood in the open doorway.

"Athena, what happened here?" Jahane asked me.

I barked at her and watched as Derrick scooped up my mom. My paw steps echoed in the eerie quiet as I followed Derrick to our room. He gently laid her on the bed and ruffled my ears as I crawled up onto the bed with her. My body inched closer to her in an effort to comfort her. I kept vigilance the whole time she slept. *Mom, it will be okay, I promise*, I kept telling her.

Jahane came in and brushed a strand of hair away from Rosie's face and settled in behind her. I moved a bit to make room for my mom's best friend. My main focus was to comfort my mom in her time of need.

After a few days Rosie finally dragged out of bed. I rolled over and watched her somberly slink off to the bathroom. Wonderful smells floated into the room and I licked my lips, but waited patiently for Rosie to return so we could eat. *Hurry, Mom. I think Jahane is cooking.*

Finally she came out and I ran out of the room behind her. The smells became more intoxicating as we rounded the corner.

Yum. As Jahane turned her back I reached up and snuck a pancake off the counter. Bacon soon followed. With the food in my mouth I quietly sauntered over to my food bowl and ate. *Wow, Jahane can cook. This is so good. I may have to get another one.*

I waited patiently for Jahane to turn her back again and gently snuck another pancake or two. I heard laughter off in the corner and looked up with a pancake dangling from my mouth. *Karl, you should try one...they are good. Wait, do spirit guides eat?*

He chuckled. *No, I don't eat anymore; but I am sure it tastes good.*

I gobbled up the last bits of breakfast and sighed, then lay down and rested my head on my paws. *Karl, Rosie is so sad...but I think she is on the mend.*

I see that. He nodded his head in the direction of the two girls. *Rosie will need to go see Marie Laveau.*

The voodoo queen. I think she came to me in a dream a few days ago.

I'm sure that was her. She is very powerful and can help her help Julian. If Rosie feels she needs to do that, you will need to be with her on this journey.

Is this Marie person a good person?

Yes and no. She will help Rosie, but Rosie must respect her and pay close attention to her. The reason Julian is in the mess he is in is because of someone lying to her. Now hurry, and don't let her forget she is to bring something to Marie.

I watched as Karl disappeared before me. Patiently I waited at the door for the girls. Rosie leaned down to me. "Thank you for being here for me."

Mom, anything for you. But don't forget the item you need to bring to Marie Laveau.

"Thank you." She ran off, and within seconds she was back. "All right, let's go."

I barked in agreement and nudged her out the door.

As we walked I knew Rosie's thoughts were all over the place...I could feel them bouncing around her head. We waited oh so not patiently for the street car to come. When it stopped I lunged in and licked the driver on the hand. He chuckled and petted me. Since we were the only three on the car I took a window seat and stuck my head out the window and let my tongue flap in the wind.

I pulled my head back in and looked at Mom. *Mom, are you okay?* She didn't answer me so I dug around in her thoughts, not surprised to find they were full of Julian. I stepped off the seat, stood in the middle, and nudged her with my head. Finally we arrived at our destination.

At the cemetery a shiver crawled along my spine. *Oh, Mom, this place looks spooky.* We trudged along until we came to a short building with marks all over it. I stayed close to my mom in case this Marie person was not good.

From the corner of my eye I saw a woman floating towards us. She looked straight at me, and in an instant I knew this was a powerful woman. I also recognized her as the woman in my dream.

"Athena, I will not hurt you." Her words were not in my head, but floated along the breeze.

I bowed my head, opened my eyes wide, and barked.

"But your witch will need your help in the coming months. Magnolia did well choosing you as Rosie's Guardian."

You knew my witch's mom?

She brought her head back and laughed silently. Her voice carried once again along the breeze. "Of course, Athena. Now I must talk to your witch."

I barked and sat beside Rosie as Marie glided towards us. As she sat beside her I scanned the cemetery and saw a man—well, not a man, because he had the face of a skeleton and a tall black hat. He tipped it at me and smiled. Ghostly figures skittered back and forth around him. He sat back on a tomb and smoke curled around him. I squinted and realized the smoke was coming from him, or the thing in his mouth. I turned back to the two women and placed my paw in Rosie's lap.

"Ah, what a beautiful Guardian you have. You must be powerful." She winked over at me and my fur rose as she lightly touched me. I refocused my attention to the man, who was now gone.

I turned back to Marie Laveau, confused. "Athena that was Baron Samedi. He is the Guardian of the dead...here to protect, much like you." Marie's voice sifted through the air.

I wondered if Rosie could hear Marie speaking to me, but it didn't seem so. The thought of this man protecting the dead made me wonder how many other human Guardians were out there. I liked that the dead had someone to protect them as well.

A breeze blew around us and I refocused my attention on my surroundings. Rosie and Jahane sat watching Marie, then Rosie spoke a spell of some sort. Before my eyes fat round objects flickered to life, with flames that danced in the air. They reminded me of the big heat box at the castle, but were smaller. Rosie and Marie spoke some more, then I saw her hand Rosie a small doll. It was amazing, and I knew I would not be playing with that one. This one belonged to my witch.

Finally we were ready to go. *Come on, Mom, let's go,* I barked out.

"All right, girl, I'm coming."

Over my shoulder I glanced back at the tombs and saw the skeleton man wave at me. "Athena, take care and protect your witch; evil is coming." Marie's voice glided over the wind towards me.

a voodoo doll and my very own ghostly server

felt a foot push me, but my eyes remained closed. My body lay sprawled on the bed—I was in my favorite "hog the bed" position. Finally Rosie's prodding made me stir. "Come on, girl." She pushed me with her foot again.

My head rolled over toward my mom, and I saw that her expression was a little sad. I knew she missed Julian. *Yes, Mom.* I stood, stretched, and then hopped out of the bed.

My paws carried me down the hall and into the kitchen, where Karl stood in the corner. *Good morning, Karl.* I filled my bowl with kibble.

Morning, Athena, Karl spoke just as Rosie came into the room. She shook her head and laughed as she watched me fill my bowl.

Mom, I would have starved if I'd waited for you.

A knock on the door pulled my attention from my breakfast. I barked and opened the door with my powers. I thought, *Wow, these powers are cool*! Then I plopped my head back down into my bowl and ate.

"Athena, you don't know who is behind the door. You should wait before you just swing it open."

Oh, Mom, you knew it was Jahane. My focus turned back to my bowl. Jahane walked over to me and petted me as I finished my food.

"Morning Athena, the wonder dog."

All of a sudden I remembered Karl was in the room. Sitting on my haunches, I looked up at him. *Karl, what are you doing here?*

Checking to see how the visit with Marie Laveau went yesterday.

It went well. Mom got a toy from the lady and fire erupted from tiny round fire boxes. I think Rosie made a deal with the lady. Do you know that Marie lady knew who I was? I said, astonished.

He chuckled. *Of course she would. Well, good...Marie's power should help Rosie on her journey.*

My feet carried me over to him. *Do you also know that they have a Guardian over the dead here?*

He nodded his head and laughed. *Yes, I'd heard rumors.*

Another knock on the door interrupted my thoughts. With my back facing it I opened the door. I turned my head and saw Andre, my mom's other friend. *Bye, Karl.* But when I turned back he was gone.

I ran up to Andre, barking.

"Hi pooch, how are you today?" He leaned down and ruffled my fur.

The gang got up. "Let's go, y'all," my mom said.

I sat outside the door wagging my tail. *Hurry, let's go.* I wondered where we were off to.

The gang, as I liked to call them, headed out the door. As we walked down the street Andre bombarded Mom with a dozen questions on witchcraft.

"Oh Andre, we will all find out more once we get to Miss Alina's."

Excitement coursed through me at the thought of seeing Miss Alina. She always had delicious treats...after all, I was getting hungry again.

At the door of Miss Alina's store I opened it and pranced inside, then headed toward the back where I knew the kind lady left my treats.

"Hello, Athena. Some special treats are waiting for you over in your spot."

I barked as she reached down and petted me. She then scooped up a silver pot and treats for the humans. My nose sniffed along the floor and over to my spot and I smelled the delicious snacks before I saw them. They were hidden but finally I found them and bit into a crunchy morsel. Laying down, I shoved them in a nice little circle to finish off the rest.

When I finished I walked around the room, and saw something in the corner that sparkled and drew my attention. I stalked the item and a little stuffed leg dangled over the table. My nose touched it and it smelled new. *Oh, no other dog has played with this. No one else's drool is on it...mine will be the first.* Carefully I pulled the little voodoo doll off the table, but quickly dropped it when I remembered the damage I'd done last time with toys. *What if this isn't for me?*

"Athena, my dear protective Guardian, that doll is for you." The voice traveled on the still air.

Gently I picked it up, the head dangling from my mouth. *It is?*

The lady from the cemetery floated over to me. Her body was now like that of my friends in the courtyard. "Yes, my dear, but it is not finished yet. With Alina's and another's help, I still have plenty of protection to add to the doll."

I softly laid it down on the floor and sat wagging my tail slowly from side to side. *But I am already a form of protection.*

She laughed silently. "Yes, but you must also have protection. I saw the way you eyed

Rosie's doll, so I figured you would like to have one of your own."

My tongue lolled out and I wagged my tail. I walked over to her and tried to nudge her hand with my head, but it went through her body.

She grinned at me as I backed up a bit. "It's okay...here."

The lady shimmered and then her body was not see through anymore. I hesitantly made my way back to her. Her soft hands felt good on my fur, and made my fur ripple against my skin.

Thank you.

"You are welcome, Guardian. As soon as I'm finished with the doll I shall bring it to you." She scooped it up from the floor and it danced in her hands. "Now run off and be with your witch." With her last words she faded from my sight.

I shook my body, then stretched and ran out of the back. As I skidded to a halt I heard that Julian had a half-brother. *Oh, hell no. Another flea bag is out there.* No one heard me.

I moved over to Rosie and lay my head in her lap. The rubbing and methodical touch of my witch's hands on me had me drifting off to sleep. The last words I heard Rosie ask were about her father, but I could no longer keep my eyes open.

I woke to wetness hitting my fur. My mom was crying. But at that moment I heard Andre snap his fingers, he'd been quiet this whole time. Both girls jumped up and Rosie wiped her face. *I think Andre is a good friend.*

"Bye, Miss Alina," I heard the three say in unison. I nudged her goodbye and leaned on her. She petted me before sending me on my way. "Bye, Athena. Don't worry, we will get your toy to you." She winked at me.

We stepped out into the bright sunlight. Andre marched down the street, and I followed him doing as he did, picking my long legs up as high as I could...being a dog and all. The streets were littered with people and we made our way through them.

"Where do you want to go eat?" I heard Andre ask.

"How about The Brackish Tavern?" Rosie spoke up. My stomach growled at the mention of food, and I eagerly followed the three down the street.

The gang stopped right in front of a restaurant, where the smells that escaped were intoxicating. I salivated as the door swung open and my nose met the most delicious aromas known to dogs.

A short round man with black hair and a mustache greeted us. When he petted me, the whiffs of food lingered on my fur. *Wow, I smell scrumptious now. Thanks, dude!*

No one noticed me walking through, though I could only guess it was because of all the food on the tables. I crawled under the table, careful not to bump anything, and saw a flash of someone blur past me. *What or who was that?* I thought as my head popped out from under the table. My stomach growled loudly and an unfamiliar face peered at me, only inches from mine. It shimmered and smiled.

Hello, furry creature. I am Lancelin, your server for today.

I looked up to see a man dressed weirdly...his clothes were pristine and he wore white gloves.

What would you like to eat? he asked, now on all fours with his head peeking at me.

A nice piece of chicken would be good. But how can you get me food? Aren't you a see through person?

He stood up and I stuck my head out from under the table. *I can do whatever I like. I have haunted....* He cleared his throat. *I mean, worked here for over one hundred years. One chicken coming up.* He turned on his heels and headed into the kitchen.

Within a few moments a plate with chicken appeared before me. *Thank you, Lancelin.*

My pleasure, furry one.

I gobbled up my chicken, licking my lips as I finished the last piece.

Later, I watched from outside as Lancelin waved goodbye to me. My thoughts plagued me on the way home, but I still kept myself on high alert.

Once back home Andre said goodbye to us, and I waited outside with Jahane while Rosie went upstairs to grab something. Out of the corner of my eye I saw a figure in a cloak. Time seemed to freeze and a growl emanated from me. *Keep away from us.*

Never. We'll have her, and soon.

The creature removed his hood, and what stared back at me was evil. Hair covered his entire body, but it quickly faded and a man who reminded me of someone stood there instead. I stepped one paw out and inched away from Jahane and closer to the creature. His canines elongated and his eyes turned black.

Who are you?

I, my dear Guardian, am one of Julian's ancestors.

What do you want with us?

That is none of your business, fur ball. But I will say this...Rosie will never get all the items on the list. I wondered what he was talking about.

As Mom came running down the stairs with something in her hand, the creature disappeared. "Come on, let's get to Madame Claudette's. I bet she has almost everything on this list."

I followed Jahane and Rosie, and kept an eye out to see if the creature returned. Once we arrived at the fortune teller's store we stepped inside, and I found a comfortable place to take a small nap. My belly was full and I was tired.

After what felt like an eternity I woke to the smell of treats. I walked over to Rosie and sniffed the bag in her hand. She reached inside and grabbed something, and in her hand was a delicious treat. I took it gently and bit into it, careful not to get any crumbs on the floor.

At the gates of the cemetery a chill ran down my spine, but I followed the two inside. As soon as I saw Marie Laveau I ran over to her and sat down.

"Hello little Guardian...or is it big Guardian now?"

Marie, I saw a creature at the house. He was pure evil. He said he would have Rosie, and she wouldn't find the last item on her list. I have no idea what he meant. He gave me the heebie jeebies, I mumbled, hoping she'd heard me.

She leaned down and whispered to me this time. "Don't worry your little furry head about this creature. I have it all under control."

Okay.

I wagged my tail and turned to Rosie. I watched as Rosie and Marie Laveau spoke, and saw the skeleton man off in the background again. He tipped his hat at me and disappeared. I also saw Marie fade out.

Rosie stood. "Come on, Jahane and Athena, let's go."

I galloped off ahead of them, chasing a few of the see through people that came out to play with me.

bourbon street and a crossroads loa

A fter a long overdue nap I woke to an empty house. Jumping off the bed, I wondered where Rosie had gone. Maybe she was in the kitchen. *Oh, food.* I zoomed out, but no Rosie. Fear came on me like a whirlwind. *Mom, where are you?*

A noise outside alerted me, so I skidded over to the door and flung it open. Rosie was getting on a loud contraption and it took off with her. I loped down the stairs, trying to catch her, but skidded to a stop at the edge of the courtyard. I stepped onto the sidewalk, but she was gone. Slowly my feet carried me away from home.

Worry erupted in me, and I felt my chest heat slightly.

No worries, Guardian, she will be fine. It may not be the best decision, but she must learn from any mistakes she makes.

I looked around and saw no one...perhaps it was a ghost. But I continued on my way down the street.

Corner after corner I turned until I ended up on a busy street full of people. They lined the streets, sloshing liquid from plastic cups and strangely shaped cups. This street, unlike the others, smelled strongly like urine and some other smell. I weaved in and out of the throngs of people.

I looked around and saw a tall woman, with blue hair and wearing a big, puffy dress, standing in front of a brightly lit building. On closer inspection, after I sniffed the air she smelled like Julian...well, without all the hair. I stepped back up onto the sidewalk, the lights drawing me closer to the woman.

The strange woman noticed me. "Hello pooch. What are you doing out here by yourself?" She looked around as if looking for someone.

I'm looking for my mom. I barked loudly, knowing she wouldn't understand if I spoke.

Before I could ask her if she had seen Rosie I was interrupted. "Eureeka, your show is about to start," a pink haired woman said as she peeked around the door.

"Coming, Philomena." She knelt down and touched my nose with the tip of her long fingernail. "Okay, pooch, you may want to get out of here before the cops come. But next time if you are with your owner you can come and see my show." She winked at me, turned, and flounced through the door.

I barked and loped off down the street. Turning one corner after another, I ended up on a street with hardly any people except for some packed into a building, from which some came out stumbling with drinks in hand. I looked up and saw a weirdly dressed man in a puffy shirt and hat. He had a beard, and held a big metal cup in his hand. I blinked and he shimmered from my sight.

Backing up, my eyes caught sight of a woman hanging from a tree down the street. But she quickly disappeared as well. *What in the world...what am I seeing?*

Further along I came to two streets crossing each other. I stood in the middle and stopped. A man came walking down the street, wearing an old straw hat and walking with a curved stick. He tipped his hat just as the man in the cemetery had. "Athena, do not be afraid of me.

I skidded to a halt. *Who are you*? I hoped he could understand me.

"My name is Papa Legba. I am keeper of the crossroads. If someone wants to speak to the loa, they must come to me first."

I hesitantly walked over to him and sniffed him. He smelled of tobacco and rum. *How do you know my name?*

He leaned his head back and bellowed out a laugh. "Of course I can understand you. I am not of this world. Oh, and Athena, every ghost and paranormal creature has heard of you. Besides, Baron Samedi said he saw you at the cemetery with Marie Laveau."

I eased back on my haunches and eyed him. *How do you know them?*

"I, like Marie Laveau, know everyone. But I'm not here for that. I have come to see the famous Guardian."

I wagged my tail and stared at him. *You wanted to see me?*

"Yes. I wanted to tell you that if you ever need me, I am here for you."

Why? I cocked my head and my ears stood taller.

"Because, Guardian, dogs are sacred to me, and the air is thick with the scent of evil."

They are?

"Yes. You especially, because you have the heightened power to see ghosts. You are a special Guardian. I heard whispers that Alexander had created one who could see ghosts, though I don't think even he knows what he's done. Athena, you are gifted by magic. A magic that is stronger than anything...the magic of love."

Before I could speak again I smelled it...the evil. The air around me swirled. Papa Legba glanced around. "Go now, Athena; head back home," he yelled.

I took off running and never looked back. *If you need me, just think of me and I'll show.*

I arrived back home with a new sense of confidence. Ghosts flitted around, welcoming me home. A young man ruffled my fur as an old woman brushed past me.

I chased and chased them until Rosie came home. I barely heard her as I ran around the courtyard. Rosie sat down on the steps, watching me play. Her laughter enticed the ghosts to turn their attention from me to her. As I tried to grab another's focus I heard Rosie fuss at one of the ghosts.

Oh, you did it now, I told him. *You must say you are sorry.* The see through man flitted back over to her with flowers in his hand. *Okay, now we will play again soon.*

The old woman ghost mouthed, *Are you sure*? *Yes.*

I bounded over toward Rosie and plopped down beside her, placing my head on her lap. She petted me. "Let's get inside."

Yes, Mom. I followed her as she went up the steps.

"Athena, I see you've made new friends."

Mom, you have no idea, I barked out.

evil has come....

Three months later

paced back and forth, sensing something bad was going on. The air stilled outside and I was on edge. When I listened to Jahane and Mom I heard something about a storm, though I was not sure what that meant. But nothing good, I guessed.

A noise in the back alerted me, and without disturbing Rosie I made my way to the back of the shop. The old man with the straw hat, along with Karl and Rosie's mom, stood staring at me as I halted. *What are you all doing here?*

Karl came over to me. *Athena, be careful tonight. We have heard whispers on the wind.*

About what?

Magnolia floated over to us. *My dear Athena, danger is on its way here. You must be prepared. You must be ever watchful.*

I started to shake. *What if something goes wrong?*

Papa Legba spoke next. He hobbled over to us, his hand clutching his walking stick. *You do your best. We will all be around to help in the aftermath.*

His strange words of an after something confused me. Magnolia waved her hand and I saw a small doll dance in the air. *My doll.*

She smiled. *Yes. Marie and I had to make sure it was blessed before actually giving it to you. Even though you have powers, we felt you needed extra protection. The air is filled with the stink of black magic.*

Thank you. I took the doll and it hung out the side of my mouth a bit.

I have added a bit of my own magic to it as well. When needed, the doll will be cloaked in invisibility so that no one can take it from you. Papa Legba leaned down and petted me.

Now go check on Rosie. I think all of her friends have gone, the three said in unison, and faded.

I sauntered out from the back and saw Rosie curled up on the sofa, so I crawled up there with her. I felt content and safe with her hands petting me.

Loud sounds came from outside...I could hear the wind howling and rain coming down. A few trash cans tumbled down the street.

Rosie removed herself from the comfy sofa and I followed. I checked every nook and cranny as she headed to the back, but an odd scent made my nose reach for the air. I sniffed and sniffed. The hairs on my back rose as magic sifted around me. Crouching low, I growled. *Who's there?*

Quickly I stalked back into the front and saw someone cloaked in black standing before me. A hood covered their face, but somehow I felt a familiarity coming from them. I barked louder.

"Dog, I have no beef with you," it spat out. "I've come for the girl."

I bared my teeth, hoping they could understand my body language. *You can't have her.*

As Rosie came running in I felt my body lifting and I flew through the air. When I hit the wall I saw another figure drop their hands, then quickly disappear.

"Athena, nooo!"

I heard Rosie's panicked screams, but couldn't move. Slowly I drifted in and out. *Am I dying?*

An eerie evil voice spoke in my head. *No, you are not dying. But after we are finished with your witch, you will wish you had.*

Once again I tried to move, but calm hands touched me. *It's over, Athena. Sleep. We will save Rosie*, Magnolia spoke in my head.

~to be continued~

A Sneak Peek
Black Magic Betrayal Voodoo Vows
Book 2

The rain pounded down on us as I was carried out of my shop. I had an instinct to wipe my hair back, but couldn't move my arms. My head bounced around as I was hoisted up by my friend...or should I say ex friend? How could I have been so blind and trusted so easily?

I was going in out of consciousness. I tried to open my eyes, but they wouldn't budge. Fear began to flow through me. What about Athena? I knew she would be worried about me. My hope was that Jahane would come to check on me, and the search would begin.

After a few moments a car door was wrenched open, the hinges squeaked, and whoever carried me tossed me roughly into the back seat of a vehicle. I sensed my kidnapper wasn't alone, but who else was there? I heard hushed whispers from two others.

Once again I tried to open my eyes. After what felt like an eternity I pried them open, but my vision was blurry. The seat dipped down a bit as someone scooted in beside me and the doors shut with a loud slam. The rain pounded down on the roof. *What in the hell are these three doing driving in a damn hurricane?* I thought.

I lay silently in the back, listening to every word. I clutched at my amulet around my neck and felt heat rise from it, protecting me. I felt the vehicle swerve and a beam of lights lit up the car. As the car swerved I slid off the seat and landed on the floorboard. Horns blew and someone screamed, "Look out! What are you trying to do, get us all killed?" I recognized that sing song voice that boomed and rattled the windows.

"Shut up, Gabby," a deep voice bellowed out. "Your minion is doing the best he can. The rain is coming down and the tread on the tires on this piece of shit are worn out. So shut the hell up."

Before the car started back onto the road, hands reached around me and grabbed me, placing me back on the seat.

"Dax, don't speak to your elders with disrespect," Gabby squealed.

Who in the hell was Dax? I tried once again to open my eyes and squinted. A figure I didn't recognize sat beside me. The car regained control and kept going.

I closed my eyes and heard the radio channels being switched, static, then a warning to stay indoors. I thought to myself, *You tell these idiots.*

"Dear sister, what will we do with her?" he asked.

Hatred bubbled up inside me as Gabby cackled. "Ah well, brother, that is for the master to decide. I know he wants her alive so he can perform the ritual. Julian has run off, so maybe if he finds out we have captured her it will bring him back into the folds of his family."

I gasped and kept my eyes shut tight. *Oh my. Julian!*

"Shh, did you hear something?" Gabby asked.

"No, she's out. But I'll go ahead and dose her again, just in case," the mysterious man sitting beside me said.

Before I could protest I felt a sting in my arm. As darkness hit me, the last thing I heard was the rain pelting against the windshield. A finger grazed my cheek before I fell into deep unconsciousness.

My body was jostled awake by the car stopping. I couldn't open my eyes but I felt someone pull me from the car, then they hoisted me up in their arms.

"Where do I take her?" the familiar voice asked.

"The master has a room set up for her."

The person carrying me jostled me in their arms, and I felt my amulet swing and make a slight contact with them. Then I felt myself falling and hit the hard ground. My hands braced my fall and I began to open my eyes.

"You idiot!"

"I'm sorry...something burned me," the familiar voice said.

I quickly hid the amulet under my shirt and closed my eyes tight. I did not want my tears or fear emerging.

Voodoo Vows

Voodoo Vows 1
Ghosts from the Past— A Voodoo
Vows Short Story
Magical Memories— A Mother's Day
exclusive Short Story

The Guardians – A Voodoo Vows Tail

Bred by Magic
Gifted by Magic

Coming Soon

Black Magic Betrayal- Voodoo Vows 2
Stone Hearts – Crescent City Sentries
Book 1

As a young girl, Diana Marie Dubois was an avid reader and was often found in the local public library. Now you find her working in her local library. Hailing from the culture filled state of Louisiana, just outside of New Orleans; her biggest inspiration has always been the infamous Anne Rice and her tales of Vampires. It was those very stories that inspired Diana to take hold of her dreams and begin writing. She is now working on her first series, Voodoo Vows.

Facebook

Goodreads

Instagram

Pinterest

Twitter

Website

Made in the USA
Columbia, SC
16 September 2022

67185627R00078